Counterplay

Dennis Norman

London | New York

Published by Clink Street Publishing 2019

Copyright © 2019

First edition.

I created this book as a work of fiction. The story and all characters are from my imagination. I used some public places and locations for the purpose of the story. Any resemblance to actual people, living or dead, or to businesses, institutions or events, are entirely coincidental.

ISBN: 978-1-913136-15-4 paperback
978-1-913136-16-1 ebook

Dedicated to Sharon, Emma, Matthew, Jonathan,
Kevin and Stephanie and all their children.
My protectors in life.

One

"What's this mum?"

Ashley was visiting his mother, Tesanee. He was in the kitchen pinching one of her freshly made spring rolls when he noticed a pile of magazines on the worktop. The top one was open, she had folded back the corner of the page.

"What's that darling?"

"This page you've earmarked in one of your magazines."

"Oh, that's something to remind me of your dad," she called from the lounge.

He picked up the magazine and joined her in the lounge, reading as he went.

"You're not seriously going to buy this, are you? Don't waste your money."

"Consider it as an investment towards our future."

"You don't need this investment. Does Karl know? It's something he would be involved in."

Tesanee took the magazine, closed the page and laid it on the coffee table.

"No, I haven't mentioned this to him yet."

"Think about it, mum. It's unbelievably expensive."

She gave him a stern look.

"I do nothing without thinking about it first Ashley, you know that. I can afford it, and I can always sell if needs be."

"Just be careful with your money mum, it won't last forever."

"Stop worrying Ashley I've been managing for a long time now."

"I know; you are good at it too. Okay if you're sure."

"I am sure now go back to work, and I'll see you for Christmas, and get something for Karl, he's not that bad."

He gave her a big hug and left.

"I will okay, bye mum."

****

Karl came home late that evening with Christmas presents. He hung his overcoat in the hall then went into the lounge to put them under the tree. He needed to warm up, so he sat in his favourite armchair to rest for a minute. The magazine was on the coffee table so he picked it up and flicked through the pages. When he saw the earmarked page he took the book into the kitchen to ask Tesanee about it.

"Hi Hun, what's this you've been looking at. Have you seen the cost of this stuff? They cost a fortune."

"I like it. It reminds me of Alex. Here, look at the website. They have quite a few valuable items."

She showed him the webpage on their laptop, which showed more details.

"I am buying something for myself as a new year present, to mark ten years since he passed. You don't mind do you, darling?"

When she told him, he thought about the cost and knew he was in trouble. She didn't have the money, but she didn't know. With the amount he'd taken from her she could, but if she tried to buy it, she would suspect him. He needed to change her mind but how could he do it?

Tesanee had known Karl for a long time. She noticed a change come over him but made light of it. Saying she was waiting until next year because she wanted to enjoy Christmas together. Ashely was coming for dinner on Christmas day.

****

Al always had sleepless nights when he needed to get up early, couldn't trust an alarm clock. For years he'd been having awful dreams about being lost and alone, searching for a way home. In some he was shopping with someone, he'd stop to look at something and when he looked around they were nowhere to be seen. He'd end up running around looking for them until he woke up disorientated and still tired.

He yawned as he showered and felt lethargic as he drank his tea. It is 6 am on a Tuesday morning at the beginning of January and he's taking his wife to the airport. His first thought was, why does she always have to catch the early flight?

He was dropping her off with her friend Jess at Gatwick Airport's south terminal where they were taking a flight to Alicante in Spain. They'd rented an apartment a short drive down the coast in Guardamar for a week.

Sonia gave him a goodbye kiss, one of those long car park ones, by the drop off bay outside the departure lounge.

"Thanks for last night, the restaurant, the dinner, the wine, the whole evening was wonderful."

"I had a great time too. Have you got everything, boarding passes, phones, lippy?"

"We've got the lot thanks, don't worry, are you sure you'll be alright while I'm away?"

"I'll be fine, I'll stop worrying if you stop fussing, call me when you arrive. Look after her Jess."

"Thanks for the lift Al, I'll look after her, make sure she doesn't drink too much, see you when we get back."

To be honest, he had no plans for the week while Sonia was in Spain. She worried about leaving him at home because he hadn't worked for four months. He'd been trying for a new assignment since the end of September but found nothing suitable. He could tell she worried about his state of mind. She always fussed every morning, calling at lunchtime and asking if he's okay in the evenings. She made lists of things for him to do during the day. He was tired of the work situation as well; it would take a small miracle to get him going again.

As he drove away, he thought, "I love driving this car on the motorway, the seats are so comfortable and they fit me perfectly, driving it is so easy." He glided along, passing other cars, their drivers on their way to work. He thought it might be a quiet day, yet another one.

So, after a cup of English breakfast tea and a bowl of cereal, he washed the bowl, emptied the dishwasher from two days ago, then settled down to read the news on his iPad and check Sonia's latest 'to-do list'. He didn't like the look of the list and wondered how he could get away with not doing it. I had better do something, he thought. He'd start with the tidying part, in other words, the easy bit. He made the bed and put all her fancy display cushions on it. An hour later Michael Bublé saved him, he was using a part of his song as a ring tone on his mobile phone. He knew the caller so just to be funny he said.

"Hi, this is Alain Dansen please leave a message after the beep and I might call you back, depends who you are."

"Stop messing around Al I can hear the radio, it's Neil, are we still on for coffee this morning?"

Al knew it was Neil from the picture on his smartphone screen, but Neil still had to tell him. This was their weekly coffee morning in Caffe Nero up the high street. They had missed the last week as it was New Year.

"Hi Neil, thank god you called I need to get out of here, and a bit of fresh air and a walk wouldn't hurt either I suppose, see you around ten."

Al had become Neil's best friend as his last one had died from prostate cancer a few months earlier. They'd known each other about twenty years now, Neil had been his agent for the first ten until he retired. Al had done some networking for the agency as well, so they had become friends.

It was good to get out of the house, and the chores, so up the high street it was. It's up hill all the way to the coffee shop and he walked. It was the only form of exercise he was getting lately. The air was always fresh this early in the year and today the sky was clear.

The smell of warm coffee hit him as he entered the shop from the cold air outside. He arrived after Neil, who was sitting at his favourite table by the window, wearing his old grey tracksuit bottoms and his Chelsea polo shirt. He'd already ordered two cappuccinos with his favourite cinnamon sprinkles on top. Al would have preferred a black Americano but he wasn't bothered, he didn't want to upset Neil. Neil had left him the chair with the view looking out of the window with his back to the counter.

"This is cosy, you got the armchairs this time, well done. What happened to your lot last week?"

"We were terrible, Spurs were two up after an hour, in total control and no way back for us, thank god for the FA cup and some joy against Peterborough."

Neil was sixty-six now and found it hard making his pension last, so Al paid. He always asked for a double stamp on the loyalty card and gave it to Neil so that once a month he could get a free coffee.

"Same for us at Arsenal but we could only draw at Bolton Wanderers."

"You'll win the replay at home."

"Yeah let's hope so. Anyway, did you catch the bus today now Percy isn't around to taxi you everywhere?"

Neil smirked at that.

"How was Christmas in Scotland by the way?"

"Scotland was beautiful, the highlands are lovely and fresh in the mornings. The hotel was great and the food was amazing."

"Show me Sonia's latest list."

Al took the list from his pocket.

"The list is not as nice though."

It was the usual stuff, cleaning and ironing, but this time the boiler needed looking at, whatever that meant. He thought it was probably the thermostat.

The Dansen's lived in a three-bedroom semi-detached chalet style house in the suburbs of south London. So that's quite a lot of cleaning as far as he's concerned.

Neil read the list while sipping his coffee.

"Any luck with the job hunting?"

Al stared out the window at the passers-by as he thought about his answer. The subject depressed him. He looked back at Neil.

"I've stopped looking Neil, it's a bit soul destroying when you keep getting turned down."

"You've always been lucky, something will turn up."

"That's may be, but I've been nicking a living for years now, so at my age, my luck is running out."

"When you get to my age you can start worrying, in the mean-time something's come up that might interest you."

This surprised Al and he put his cup down to listen.

"I thought you'd retired from the agency."

"I still keep in touch but this one's not through the agency it's a personal thing."

"What's going on, has Sonia spoken to you to get me going again, I worry about her because she worries about me so much."

"No, she doesn't know, and it's up to you if you tell her. I hope you don't mind but I've invited someone to join us today."

Al couldn't bear the suspense.

"Oh who?"

"He's sitting over there."

Al looked around in the direction Neil had pointed and saw coffee drinkers sitting at their laptops using the free internet. Neil waved to a dark-haired, smartly dressed young man sitting by himself near the counter and beckoned him over. He came to join them and offered his had to shake.

Al had two thoughts as they shook, he looks to be in his mid-twenties, and I think I recognise him.

"Hello, Mr Dansen."

"Hi, I vaguely remember your face but I'm sorry I can't remember your name."

"It's Ashley, don't you remember him?" Neil said.

"You're joking, not Alex's son surely, I haven't seen you for over ten years."

"Yes, it's Ash now though and It must be nine years because that's when dad died."

"Well you've grown, sorry I suppose you would have by now. it's nice to see you, do you still live around here?"

"I have a flat, it's about ten minutes' drive away but I've still got a few mates here so I'm often back."

"I haven't seen you in here before, how have you been getting along?"

"Alright, thanks. I have something that needs solving. Neil said you're good at locating things and you're not working now, so I would like to discuss it with you."

"Right, what's on your mind."

"I don't want to discuss it here in the coffee shop, will you come to my place this afternoon?"

"I don't mind listening but I'm not sure you know what I do for a living now. Anyway, what is so secret that we can't discuss it here?"

Ashley looked pensive as if he was making up his mind whether Al was the right person to help him.

"It's a bit sensitive, a family thing, you remember mum and I don't like eavesdroppers."

"Okay, I get that, but I'm a bit busy with housework at the moment. Get us another coffee and I'll think about it, we're having cappuccinos with cinnamon sprinkles."

Ashley went to the counter to get their coffees. Al turned to Neil.

"What's going on."

"'I'm busy with 'housework', don't make me laugh. Look, I don't know the ins and outs but he approached me in the supermarket yesterday, and asked if I knew where to find you."

Al was honestly surprised. "Me, why would he want my help?"

"I must admit I hardly recognised him, but when he introduced himself, I told him he was in luck, and that I usually see you in Nero's for coffee this morning, he said he'd see us today."

"What do you think, should I go and listen to what he wants?"

7

"Well, what else have you got going on except housework?"

"Yeh, housework and no assignment at the moment, I do need something to occupy me while Sonia is away, I dropped her at Gatwick earlier, she's off to Guardamar in Spain for a week with Jess."

"Good for her, I wish I was going too."

"You just want to go with Jess."

"That's not fair I haven't had a holiday for a few years and somewhere hot sounds nice." He looked up to see Ashley on his way back. "He's coming back."

Ashley returned with three drinks on a tray, sat down and they started reminiscing. Neil sat quietly, listening, while Al and Ash chatted.

"The first time I saw you, you were a shy five-year-old, you hid in the back room with your mum. It was in The Hague I'd come to your house to offer your dad a job, do you remember?"

"Sort of, I was a bit young then and I've always been shy, mum would have hit me with her wooden spoon if I'd interrupted you. My mum is old fashioned in that way, children should be seen and not heard."

Neil had a look of disbelief on his face.

"What on earth."

"Yes, she was pretty strict with me in those days, I had become nosey she would say, I only had a couple of friends and I didn't mix socially with the other kids at the nursery school, so I was just inquisitive at home I suppose."

"Well, I'm sorry to hear that, I did see her scolding you more than once, is she alright?"

"No, she's not, that's what I want to talk to you about, but not here."

"Alright, Ash if it's something to do with your mum give me your address and I'll come over later."

"Thanks, Mr Dansen." He gave Alain a business card with his name, mobile number and address on.

"Hey if I'm calling you Ash then you can call me Al, as we're old friends."

Al called the number on Ashley's business card. Ashley stored Al's number in his phone contacts. Then he stood, shook both their hands and left them to talk it over.

"Don't start, I'll go and listen to his problem, but I'm not going to be shilled into some nonsense project."

"Come on, he's obviously worried and struggling to get any help, he needs someone familiar with the family and you understand both him and Tesanee."

"Well I have known them for a long time, and I liked his dad no end, I'll help him if I can, but you know what my job's like, projects pop up all the time."

"I know, but while you're not busy you might as well listen and see if there's something you can do."

"Right, I'm off I'll call you later and let you know if I need your help."

Two

Al hurried back down the hill in half the time it took to walk up, his collar pulled up to stop the wind swirling around his neck. The wind was blowing downhill with him and there was a winter chill in the air.

He was just hanging his coat up in the hall when his phone chirped, it was a text from Sonia telling him she had arrived safely and asking if he was okay. He went through to the breakfast room, sat on a bar stool where he replied he was and not to worry, to enjoy herself and he'd call her in a few days. He didn't tell her about Ashley.

He checked Sonia's list again, then made himself a sandwich. While he ate it, he thought about Ashley and his mum and wondered what he could want. After eating his lunch, he sent a text to Ashley telling him he was on his way. Ashley replied almost instantly asking him to ring the bell and he would open the main door.

He found Ash's block tucked away at the end of a tree-lined cul-de-sac with a turning circle. There were plenty of parking spaces, he assumed at this time of day, most people would have driven to work. He parked and walked towards the building. He saw the buzzer pad showing every number on a plate by the main door. Ash lived at number ten and after being buzzed in he climbed the four flights of stairs to the top floor.

Ash watched Al climb the stairs from the top of the stairwell and when he arrived he stood aside to let him in.

"Hi Al, come in, I've got the top floor."

Al took a deep breath. "Shame there's no lift."

He soon understood he meant the entire top floor, including next door. The two apartments had been combined to form something resembling a penthouse, with windows all around one side with a view to die for. You could see most of London at 180 degrees.

Inside it was extremely modern compared to the exterior. There had been extensive changes to the design. Al immediately thought he had made it into a futuristic place whereas it was pretty current actually.

Ashley had changed his clothes and was dressed casually in white chinos and a white polo shirt. He had a blue sweater draped across his shoulders. He was proud of his flat and he proceeded to show off some of his additions.

"Watch this, close the curtains."

The blinds closed automatically to the sound of his voice.

"Open the curtains," and they opened again. "Everything is remotely controlled."

"So, this is one of those speech-controlled systems I've seen advertised, a bit flash isn't it?"

The kitchen was spotless, almost clinical, all white units and dark marble worktops. Every gadget you could think of was on display. There was an Apple laptop sitting on a breakfast bar. Al thought, I bet he's adept with a computer, from the earliest days of the internet his dad would have shown him around.

"Welcome to my humble abode, mum bought it for me; coffee?"

"Humble abode, I'm a bit shocked actually, she must have got a big payout from the sale of dad's company to afford this, and something for herself, and yes I'd love a coffee."

"Filter, pod or instant? Both partners got an equal share, that's mum and Kit."

"Pod's fine, so where is she now? Mum I mean."

He had one of those super-duper coffee machines with pre-filled pods, so he made two cappuccinos with cinnamon sprinkles and he also put some biscuits on a plate then went on to explain she had moved away to a small town about twenty-five miles south midway between here and the coast.

He must have a cleaner, Al thought, maybe I could get them to come and clean our place.

"Thanks for this, I don't usually drink cappuccino, only when Neil gets me one, I don't like to upset him though it's his only coffee of the week."

"Want me to change it?"

Al took a seat by the window and looked across the landscape towards London.

"What, no this is fine. Is mum on her own down there?"

"She is now."

He turned back to look at Ashley. "Oh! you said this was something to do with her, so go on spit it out and I'll listen."

Al had read somewhere, probably in some crime novel, the secret was listening, you have to let people talk naturally, so you could get an idea of what you're in for, let them get to it in their own time. So he sat back to listen.

"She's living with this bloke. His name is Karl. I think they met at the pub where mum was cooking. Anyway, he came along about a year after dad died, mum still needed a shoulder to cry on and he was there."

"Last I heard she was cooking Thai food at the Grapes."

"She was for a while, then she worked for Romaine, do you remember him?"

"Of course, he was my cousin's mate who did weddings and outdoor social events, a nice man who always had time to help people out."

"You mean your cousin Drew, I met him a few times."

"Yeh, that's him."

Al stopped listening for a minute and his mind wandered to the time he had worked with Alex. He blinked and realised he'd missed something Ash had said.

"Sorry, Ash I was thinking about the old days, what was that?"

Ash backtracked and carried on with his story.

"Look, Alain, I was sixteen when dad died, and I was angry about it because I thought he was in good health at the time. He was out cycling most days, looking trim and the perfect weight. Then he goes and dies, they said it was from cancer.

"Well, I didn't know he had it let alone die from it. I didn't believe it then and I still don't. Okay, it might have been the cause, but he must have had it under control, it was as if we'd all forgotten he even had it."

"Please call me Al, Ash. It's a serious illness Ash and people do die from it."

"I know but it was so sudden I think someone caused it."

"You're not serious, the end of his life was marked with health problems. it was natural causes you must believe that."

"I'm deadly serious."

He paused, sipped his coffee and nibbled a biscuit He seemed slightly nervous.

"What's up you seem nervous, it's normal to be nervous, Ashley. Anyone in this situation would be nervous, carry on."

"Dad was doing really well with his cancer and had control of his drug dosage. Mum had been helping him with the treatment even when I was young. She was petrified of losing him like some of her friends in Singapore. So, she put him on a diet, and it worked he lost about four stone."

"Tell me why you think someone assisted his death."

"Soon after Karl came on the scene I was going to college. I was too wrapped up in my studies to notice what they were doing. Anyway, when you're sixteen you don't want to be around your mum, do you? He was romancing her the way dad used to do, they were so in love, mum and dad I mean. To my mind, he only wanted to take advantage of us.

"Karl was a bit younger than dad and she liked him a lot I could tell. I wasn't sure though, but I thought it was pretty natural for me to get upset that he was taking mum away."

"Hey, hold on, don't you think it was hard for her without your dad?"

Ashley thought about that then carried on.

"She was happy, but I couldn't see that, and It seemed I was looking on from a distance. I had exams and wanted to be left alone but he kept having a go at me, it was as if he wanted me out. I was just a kid and mum did everything for me. At that time in my life, I was just like every other sixteen-year-old boy, not the tidiest."

Ashley was being completely honest, but Al couldn't help stopping him.

"Think about it, she needed you to help her out by contributing to the home a bit more."

"I was grieving as well, and she wasn't being nice to me then. You know what she was like when I was young."

"I can understand that you were still young and trying to deal with it in your own way, but she must have been lonely and there's you being stroppy."

"Do you want to know why I want your help or not?"

"Sorry, it was a long time ago and you've had a hard time too."

"It was a stressful time for mum, what with the funeral and taking over dad's part of the company. She inherited his shares you know and became a partner. Albeit a silent one."

He looked away as if he was going to cry.

"Will you excuse me a minute I need to use the bathroom."

While he was away, Al texted Neil to say he was at Ashley's and could he see him later. He thought he might need someone to talk it over with.

Ashley returned so he pocked his phone and waited for him to continue.

"Where was I, oh yes. She told me Karl was a regular at the pub. He kept asking the landlord about her, and he told him, she had just lost her husband. So, he started to talk to her, and she thought he was a nice guy, caring you know.

"So she liked him?"

"He was a sly one."

"In what way?"

"I reckon he fancied her before dad died. He was waiting for the right moment if you know what I mean. So, as I said before he romanced her for about three months before asking her out. It's not frowned upon where we come from to move on, quickly as it were."

"Are you implying he had something to do with your father dying."

"I wasn't thinking like that at first because I locked myself away and tried to hide from it all, but after a while, he got under my skin and I suppose I got under his, then I started to get suspicious."

"Paranoid more like it, it's obvious he liked her and when he saw her upset or sad, he wanted to console her, nothing wrong with that."

"He just wouldn't leave her alone though."

"She didn't want to be alone, she wanted company and he provided it."

"He was swamping her, she needed to grieve."

"Calm down let's have another drink you're getting upset, how about some water my coffee is tepid now anyway."

"I'll get it, let me think."

While he was away Al took a walk around the flat and got to thinking too, what if he wasn't paranoid and Karl had planned a way of getting her to himself. He called out.

"Hold on a minute it's hard for me to see Karl killing your dad so he could be with your mum and also getting rid of you too."

Ashley returned with two glasses of water.

"I'm not sure either but he was certainly on the scene quickly afterwards."

"Well, even if it's true you'll never prove it now; it's been nearly ten years."

"I know but I thought you would need some background information. That's not why I asked you to come over today."

Al looked at Ashley with suspicion written all over his face.

"I thought it was something other than you didn't like him. Has something else happened?"

15

'Yes, he's stolen all her money."

This was like a gut punch and Al felt it knock the wind out of him.

"I can't believe that, how do you know?"

"He's been gradually shifting it into his bank over a period of a few years now."

"You're not joking are you how can you know that?"

"It's a long of a story."

Al took a sip of his water, leaned back in his chair and thought, what the hell am I in for here? I can't believe I'm hearing this.

"Let's hear it then, I'm not going anywhere."

"If you don't mind me explaining."

"Before you start, what's his surname?"

"Hurnston."

"So, it's Karl Hurnston?"

"Yes."

"Well, you'd better carry on. It's a good job I'm not busy. When did this start?"

"I started to get interested in him when I was at college. He seemed to be asking a lot of questions about dad. I overheard him once asking mum if she knew what dad did at work. She said it was to do with computers, but she didn't know the specifics. As far as I knew he'd always worked with them since she met him."

"Yes, he was a genius with all types of computer."

Ashley took his time, stood and walked around the room, and drank some water before continuing.

"I know he was, he was my idol, the things he created. He would come home all proud and show me what he'd done. It was always a joy to see his smile after he had cracked some code.

"Anyway, I thought something wasn't right, but I wasn't sure what and I when asked mum she told me I was imagining it and if something was, she would tell me. I knew she wouldn't because it wasn't her way."

"Not many computers in her village in the Philippines."

"She had been brought up to be proud and keep an outward

look of control but inside she was not happy. Karl was becoming a bully and she wasn't about to admit it to me. I heard the arguments and caught a few words, but I still couldn't make sense of it."

"Did you tell her what you'd heard?"

"No way. I started to make little recordings when the rowing started and then I'd listen to them at night before I went to sleep. I had dreams of them splitting up and me and mum getting back to normal again if you could call it normal."

"You were spying on them and recording it?"

Ashley ignored the question.

"In some of the recordings he asked her for money to help his business, and sometimes she agreed."

"So, she lent him some."

"Not always, when she said no, he would lose his temper and raise his voice, it sounded like he and almost hit her a few times, but I don't think he ever did."

"Are you sure he never hit her?"

This question shocked Ashley.

"What, no, I don't think he did. Mum would have said. I decided to try and keep an eye on her finances though, to help her really. It wasn't easy, she was secretive where money was concerned."

"How did you do that, exactly?"

"Dad had opened me a bank account when I was thirteen and mum had put a good amount in it when I went to college. I pretended I needed a bit more and picked a moment when she couldn't get to the bank. She gave me her bank details if I promised to forget them straight after. Which I did after I made a note of them."

"So, you kept a watch on her transactions after that?"

"Yes, I knew which bank she used and decided to get a job there after college. I worked hard that year and made the grades, then after graduating I applied and got a bank telling job at her branch. I used my college work together with my banking exams and got promoted to the IT department."

"Well done, your dad would be proud of you."

"Thanks, I always wanted to make him proud. Anyway, this allowed me to access accounts and one was my mum's. You're not supposed to access family stuff but I'm a pretty good hacker nowadays. Probably got it from dad, he was a great programmer before he died."

"You're right there, he could learn any package quickly. He wrote fantastic great programs."

"It took me a few years but I'm now at head office and I can monitor her account in secret. I saw small amounts going out and followed them all. One stood out and was more frequent than the others.

"This leads me to Karl's account. It started small and got a little bit bigger until there was more going out than coming in. Her fortune was dwindling away slowly, and she didn't see it until it was too late. She'd had so much that she stopped worrying about money and probably thought it would last forever and it still might but that's not the point."

"Jesus Ashley, that's a hell of a story. What do you want me for?"

"I want it back and I'm asking for your help. I can see where it's gone but I can't get near his account and even if I could I couldn't steal it without it showing up. I need help with a plan. I remember dad telling me you were the one with all the ideas. So, could you please help me. I can only monitor I can't actually get near the money."

"And you want me to get it for you. How were you thinking of me doing that?"

"I have all of dad's database coding from his computers and I've doctored it to be used in the banking industry. He always used to tell me, *when they give you something to use, use it.*"

"I remember what he was doing but how does it work now?"

"It's still a tracking software but I can follow Karl's banking anywhere he uses it, his debit or credit cards even if he's online, either by a computer, iPad or mobile phone."

"So, you've created some hacking software."

"You could call it that, I call it *Counterplay*."

"Is that the name or your play on the revenge scenario?"

"It's my name for the program, we can call it that, it's a good name, what do you think?"

"We? Well yes, it's great but what can I do?"

"He has disappeared, simply gone, I want you to help me find him and then we'll see about getting my mum's money back."

Al sat back and thought a while. This was not what he expected. I'm not a detective, he thought, I'll have to think about this.

"How long has he been gone?"

"A week now."

"If you can monitor his card transactions you should be able to locate him yourself."

"Kind of, but I can't be the one who confronts him he knows me, and I can hardly get him to part with mum's money just like that. Have a think about it, I'll get us another drink."

While he was away Al thought about what Ashley wanted him to do. He thought long and hard, then he had an idea. When Ashley returned Al asked him straight out.

"Okay let me get this straight, you want me to chase around looking for him and then what? Look there's a lot to think about and I need to go and do just that. I'm interested because of your mum. Does she know what you're doing by the way?"

"What! no way, she has no idea what I'm doing."

"Ashley she's obviously proud of you and the career you've chosen but she has no idea why. Do you enjoy your job or is this obsession leading you?"

"It's a bit of both really. I want to look after her, for dad."

"I need to go home and think about this, I'm not convinced I can help. Give me the night to come up with something."

They finished their drinks and Al rose to leave.

"Fine, you'll let me know then?"

"Yes! I'll call you tomorrow."

Three

Al had arrived at Ashley's feeling intrigued and left feeling shocked. He couldn't believe what Ashley had told him. The last time he had spoken to Tesanee she had not hinted that her partner was like that. I just need to talk to him, he thought, and we'll solve this in no time. Ashley is probably overreacting. It left him wondering where to begin. He knew he was in though; it was what he needed at this time in his life. A good mystery to solve. Keep his brain ticking over. Better than doing Sudoku puzzles to pass the time All those logic problems he'd been doing were going to help. A change from copying and pasting each day, same old same old.

He arrived home with an inkling of an idea for how he was going to approach the problem. He certainly couldn't do it alone though and he couldn't do it for free either.

He called Ashley back.

"Hi, Ash if I'm going to help, I'm sorry to ask but I need some sort of payment. I can't pay out for travelling around much."

"Wow is that a yes? No problem I'll get you some expense money. Give me your bank details and I'll transfer some."

"With your skills, I'm not happy about you checking out my bank."

"What! you don't trust me?"

"I'm just wary of anyone. I hope you don't take offence, I'm always suspicious."

"Don't worry I'm not going to touch your bank account."

"Right I'll text you the numbers. I'll get back to you about anything else."

After mulling it over for a while he decided to call in the services of his little big brother. The phone rang a few times then went to answerphone, he left a message to call him urgently. Far too much to explain in a message.

Next, he called Neil, who answered after two rings.

"Hi Al, how did it go?"

"I'm in and now I need to work out how to help him. You could help too if you don't mind. Can you keep your phone handy I'm going to be moving around a bit and I don't want Ashley to know exactly what I'm doing, so I need a person here to liaise with, as a sort of a PA, maybe organise some stuff for me?"

"I'd love to Al and it's all very well but what about my phone bill?"

"Thanks, Neil, you were always the best on the phone working for that recruitment agency and don't worry about the bill, I'll get you a phone to use and pay the account when this is over."

"Well alright then if you're sure."

"Ash is going to have to pay I can't be doing this for nothing."

While Al waited, he settled down to a bit of planning. Firstly, how to begin the search? Even though Ash didn't want his mum to know about what he had been doing he needed to talk to Tesanee about Karl. Ash made him sound like a nasty piece of work, and he wanted to find out more about his background. It would help if he knew Karl's habits, therefore he needed an excuse to see her.

He started to day dream about when he'd first met her when Michael Bublé roused him. It was his brother Toby ringing back.

"Hi Tobe, how's Jo?"

"She's fine, how are you and Sonia doing, what's up?"

"We're okay, she's in Spain until next week. How are you fixed at the moment I need a minder for a few days, maybe longer?"

"What, she's gone without you are you sure everything is alright?"

"Yes, she's gone with her mate Jess, I dropped them both at Gatwick this morning."

"That's good I'll tell Jo." Al heard Toby's wife Joanne call out. "Who's that?"

"Alain's on the phone. Sorry Al, what's it about?" He paused then said, "I've been really busy, but anything for you, is it urgent?"

"You could say that. I've been asked to help out an old friend. If you can come over, I'll tell you about it, not over the phone."

"It had better be urgent, Joanna is all over me at the moment, she watches my every move. You could be in luck though I'm working part-time now. I'll phone work and check my rota and call you back, give me ten minutes."

Al used the time to run an internet search for Karl. Not much to be found though, a secretive guy with no Facebook, Instagram or Twitter accounts.

When Toby called back Al was hoping he could help.

"Hi Al, I'm all yours for a week, I asked for some time they owed me, and they agreed, and I've explained it to with Jo. now, what's it all about?"

Al ignored his question.

"How long till you get to me, can you get a flight asap, I'll pay, I'm getting expense money up front." At least he hoped he was, he knew he was cheap but he's not doing this for free.

"Blimey it does sound urgent I'll get online and book for this evening, text me your card details, there are usually seats on Ryanair or Aer Lingus from Dublin to Gatwick, I'll be with you later or first thing tomorrow."

He texted Toby the bank details and within ten minutes Toby called back to say he was catching the Ryanair red-eye tomorrow morning and would be arriving at a quarter past eight. Hand luggage only

"Great, text me the flight number and I'll see you at the airport."

Wonderful he thought, his second early morning trip to Gatwick Airport in two days. This time to pick up.

****

He texted Sonia when he crawled into bed that night. Humming to himself as he typed. I'm missing you and the bed is massive without you in it. I hope you are having fun. It seems like I might be a bit busy while you are away.

The dream was back that night, but he was pretty worn out from the early start and the revelations of the day, so it didn't last, and he slept quite well actually.

The next day he was up early, shower, cup of tea all done and on his way to Gatwick when his phone pinged. It was Toby texting to say he'd landed and would be waiting outside by the pick-up point to save him parking.

It was mild over the south of England that morning and Toby had been waiting about ten minutes when Al arrived. He flicked the boot open from the switch inside the car and Toby dumped his bag then climbed into the passenger seat. His long legs were so cramped in the small two-door cabriolet, he had to push the seat back as far as it would go to get comfortable.

"Morning bruv, it's cold out there, you said asap."

They bumped fists.

"Morning, you're damn right, I haven't been up this early two days running for a long time. I'm sorry about the head height but I'm keeping the roof up, you're right it's absolutely freezing out there."

He gave his brother a long look.

"Jesus Toby that is a serious haircut for this weather." He had gone for a short back and sides.

I like his woollen jacket though, just right for January, thought Al.

"Get real, it's the fashion, Al. Anyway, what have you done that needs my help?"

"It's a little bit of business for an old friend's son."

"Dangerous?"

"No, we just need to get something back for him."

"Where from?"

"I don't know yet we need to find it first."

"Ooh! A puzzle I love a good puzzle."

"Just keep your riddles to a minimum I know most of them anyway."

"I've got plenty of new ones for you don't worry."

"It's a big puzzle this one, there's a lot to find out, maybe too much."

"But you won't know until you start looking into it, maybe we won't need to know too much."

"There's never too much information with something like this."

"Have you called Rob and Phil?"

"No, we won't need them for this."

"Do they know?"

"No, I haven't told them."

"What happened to the team, brothers in arms and all that? They are going to find out sooner or later."

"Let's leave it for later, shall we? It's a two-man job."

During the drive, Al outlined most of what Ashley had told him and what he wanted from them. Toby listened attentively and gave a few ifs and buts. They dropped by Neil's house on the way to give him one of Al's WorldSim dual phone adapters. He was up and eager to help.

"Hi Neil, meet Toby, Toby meet Neil, we can't stop long so here is the phone I was on about, this is a dual sim adapter, I don't expect you to know all about it but it's like a phone with a sim in it, it links to your phone via Bluetooth. When I call the number, your phone will ring and any calls you make will go on my bill. It means we're not using your phone number Okay? Give me your phone and I'll set it up for you."

Al downloaded the app to Neil's phone and connected the two.

"You young un's and your fancy phones. So, when I want to

call you I press the app and the phone will act like mine but use the adapter, is that right?"

"Perfect, you're not just a pretty face after all. I've added my number onto your favourites, it's at the top so you can find it easily, got it?"

"Got it."

"We've got to go so I'll call you if I need you."

"Be careful out there."

****

They arrived home and Al offered Toby a cup of coffee. Sonia and Al only had decaf at home and Toby didn't care for it, but he decided he wasn't going to look a gift horse in the mouth.

"Wow, you've changed the place a bit since I was last here."

"Yes, a bit of structural work and the back room is much bigger, we love it."

They chatted about their personal lives for about half an hour while they drank their coffees, then Al explained that he planned for Karl to give them all of Tesanee's money without him knowing anything about it. Even though he didn't know all of it yet. He also had a present for Toby.

"Here's a little something for you."

"Ooh, a present."

"Stop it. It's this watch, it's a 'Timewerk', it has a camera that can take HD photos and video with night vision."

"Amazing, is that all?"

"You don't want much do you, as a matter of fact, it's also got a microphone for audio recordings. Then you can download them all via a USB cable."

"All that lot, and with a leather strap."

"Come on, it's important."

"I know, what are you wearing these days?"

"Not my usual, this is an 'Aviator' it's a smart pilot. It communicates with my smartphone, it displays calls, texts, email, social media, and my calendar if I set it all up."

"You're a right Mr. Gadget Man, aren't you? Anything else for our surveillancing?"

"It tracks your steps and sleep, not that I'm getting much. I've got the Go-Pro waterproof camera too."

"Tell me, why are you helping him?"

"I liked his dad, I like him, and his mum. I helped them before so why not again, I'm not doing much else for the moment."

Al's phone stopped them, Michael Bublé again.

The screen lit up and Al answered.

"This is Dansen."

"Hi Alain, it's Ashley. Mum called, she's met Karl at a fast food restaurant and he's threatening her, she needs help. Can you come?"

"Where is she, Ash?"

"Wych Cross near East Grinstead at a McDonald's, she's outside in her car in the car park with the doors locked."

"What car does she drive Ashley?"

"It's an Audi A3 cabriolet, but the roof will be up."

"Colour?"

"It's white."

"What about Karl?"

"He's got a black BMW M3."

"Okay tell her to stay put and we'll come and get her."

"We, who's with you? I want to come too."

"My brother is with me. There's no need for you to come she will understand when she sees me."

"No, I want to come I'll need to explain to mum. Come and get me."

Ashley was upset and sounding hysterical. Al needed him to be calm and receptive.

"Hey, calm down, we'll pick you up if you insist. We'll be ten minutes getting to you." Al closed the call.

"Come on Tobe we need to get moving that was Ash, his mum needs help."

"I heard, she should call the police we aren't cut out for this."

"I told him I'd help and that includes you now."

"Give me the keys and you can map read. I can't be a passenger in your car. You are a terrible driver."

They dropped everything and rushed out to Al's car. Al directed Toby to Ash's apartment. When they were close Al texted Ashley and he was waiting by the door when they arrived. Al had to get out to let Ashley get in the back of the two-door car. After picking him up they sped away to find Tesanee. Al introduced them both.

"Toby this is Ashley; Ashley this is Toby."

"How come Toby is here?"

"I thought we might need a little help, so I invited him along."

"What are you, a partnership?"

"I told you he's my brother, we worked together on and off for a few years until he went off to Ireland. We always stay in touch; we can get to each other in short notice."

"Ireland. Were you visiting or is this a special trip?"

"Al called me last night."

"Did you come over this morning?"

"Yes, on the first Ryanair flight from Dublin."

"That was quick thanks for helping out."

"I haven't done anything yet son, we'll see if I'm any help later on. The last time I came over to help Al I was his best man, he was getting married. Again."

This is all well and good thought Al but they needed to get moving.

"Toby shut up and drive, I keep going up and down this road lately, I've already been near there this morning, it's not far from Gatwick airport."

Toby had made his way back to the main road.

"Which is the best way?"

"Head for Gatwick, down the M25 then off on the A22. Then keep going, it's about forty-five miles from here. The A road is one lane and slow. With the traffic, it will probably take us around an hour and a half."

Four

They pulled up in the restaurant car park next to Tesanee's Audi. She was sitting in Karl's BMW, which was parked on the other side of hers. Everybody got out at the same time. Karl was yelling at Tesanee as she walked away towards Ashley.

He called after her and grasped the tail of her coat to hold her, but she squirmed aside him. Shouting at him as she ran.

"Get away from me."

He was quick to kick out at her. Until Al came up behind him and put his arm around his shoulder to stop him.

Calling out. "That's enough."

Karl was having none of it.

Shouting. "Get off me," as he spun around. "Who are you anyway?"

Al started to speak. "We only want to…"

Karl thrust him back. As he fell backwards he caught Karl's left arm, and they went tumbling onto the ground between the cars. Karl landed on top of Al who smacked his head on the kerb. Karl punched out with his free arm and caught Al's cheek. Toby ran over and grabbed at Karl to pull him off Al Tesanee screamed and started to cry, Ashley was shouting as Toby struggled in the small gap.

Toby had just pulled Karl up and they heard, "Oy! what's going on?"

Al pushed himself up onto his knees.

A member of the restaurant staff had come outside to see what was going on. Karl pushed free from Toby and ran to his car. He slid in quickly, started it, and almost hit Al as he reversed, swinging out of the parking space as he drove away. Al scrambled to his feet and Toby eased him up.

The restaurant guy came forward.

"Come inside, I'm the manager here, I was watching, so I saw it all, we've got it on CCTV."

Toby helped Al, and they walked into the restaurant with the manager. He led them to a table by the rear wall where the four of them sat to catch their breath. Toby chose a seat with his back to the wall, looking towards the exit. Tesanee and Ashley faced him.

The manager showed concern and signalled a waitress.

"Get them all drinks." He looked at Al. "It looks like you need to clean yourself up, the toilets are through that door."

He pointed to a door in the back wall. Then he turned and went through a door marked 'Staff'. The waitress asked.

"What can I get you?"

They all asked for coffee and Al asked for a glass of water too. She scurried off to arrange the drinks. Al washed his face and hands in the restroom and checked himself while the others sat and tried to calm down. They talked about what had just happened. Ash's concern was Karl had hurt his mum, but she assured him she was okay. The manager came with their drinks and said he'd called the police. Al was walking back towards the table when Toby looked up and shouted.

"He's back."

Al turned and looked at Karl in the doorway searching for them. When he saw them, he came in, but the manager shouted.

"Oy! you are not allowed in here I saw what you did, and we have it on film, so go."

"I want to explain," said Karl.

Al walked towards him and calmly said.

"Just go. Can't you see she's upset, and you've hurt her."

It was so quick he never saw the punch coming. Karl caught him with a right hook on the cheek and he went down like a sack of potatoes. Out like a light. He put his hand out to steady himself but caught the side of their table. Cups went crashing down, but he never knew what happened next.

Al was under the table, leaning against the wall, out cold. Ash and Tesanee moved the table, they tried to pull him up when a customer having lunch with his children came over to offer assistance.

"I'm a police officer, off duty at the moment, don't touch him, somebody had better call an ambulance."

The waitress brought a mop to clean up the mess then left to get Al another glass of water. Al's frameless glasses had cut his cheek under his left eye, blood was running down his face onto his shirt, the waitress brought a towel to soak it up and try to stop the bleeding. He'd hit the back of his head on the table as he fell making him groggy and he'd sat in the water from the spilt glass.

He'd come round and drank a few sips of water when the ambulance arrived five minutes later at the main doors.

He looked at Ashley. "What the hell just happened, was I out?"

"Karl knocked you out, then Toby chased him out to his car, and he drove off again."

Two ambulance crew lifted him under the arms into the back of the ambulance and a lady paramedic cleaned his wound. She stuck paper strips on his cheek and told him to rest. She advised him to go to the hospital, but he wanted no more fuss, so he promised her he'd be alright. They gave him a couple of pain killers and told him not to drink alcohol today.

More drinks arrived, Tesanee was wiping her nose and sobbing. The back of her coat was dirty from Karl's dirty shoes. She kept apologising to everybody until Toby explained she wasn't to blame for Karl's behaviour.

"That will be a chinner by tomorrow."

Toby laughed.

"You mean a right shiner."

Al didn't think it was funny. "Why am I so stupid; I should know by now I'm crap at this fighting lark. I didn't see that coming, I only wanted to talk to him."

Toby wouldn't let him forget it.

"You never laid a glove on him either."

The ambulance crew left, and they sat in silence for a while.

Al thanked the off-duty Police officer for his help, then he went to the manager and thanked him for calling the ambulance. A few minutes later the police arrived. A policewoman came to talk with them while a policeman spoke with the manager.

She addressed Toby "Could you tell me what happened?"

She wrote it on her pad as they told her.

"Do you know the man who did this?"

Al looked up towards the exit and pointed. "Him."

He was still seeing double but was he was seeing things too? Karl had returned.

The policewoman turned "Who?"

Al was astounded. "He's at the door, I can't believe he came back again."

She called her colleague who left the manager, dashed over, grabbed Karl by the arm and escorted him to a table away from the others.

Al stood to confront him.

The policewoman put her arm over his. Stopping him before he left the table.

"Leave it, my colleague will deal with him, but I need to ask, did you provoke him to do this?"

Al's anger hadn't abated.

"What! he knocked me out and you think it's my fault."

"That's not what I'm saying."

"Well, it sure sounds like it."

"Okay, well we've got him now, so I suggest you go home and rest, is there somebody to drive you?"

"Yes, Toby can take me."

"You must report to the station to make a full statement within the next seven days."

"I'll try to come tomorrow after I've cleaned myself up."

"Where is the station?" Asked Toby.

"East Grinstead police station."

She packed up her notes and getting ready to leave. "Is there anything else because that's it for us, we're finished here. I advise you to go straight out, don't talk to anybody on your way."

She'd packed her things and stood to go and said, "And bring id."

Ashley stood up with his mother and led her towards the door. Tesanee kept asking him how Al came to be there, but he told her he would explain on their way home. Al and Toby hadn't even had time to talk to her, but Ashley wanted to get her away from there as quickly as he could.

Toby called out goodbye and Al shouted to Ashley he would call him in the morning.

"To see where we go from here."

They watched as Ashley drove away.

Toby helped Al to the car "Come on let's go."

The policewoman joined her colleague so they could speak to Karl together.

****

Karl knew he was in trouble as soon as he saw the police officers. He hadn't expected them to be there. He'd only come back to explain, but he shouldn't have bothered. There was no time to run and what is the point of arguing with the police, so he sat patiently with his head in his hands waiting to be questioned. While his mind whirled.

How the hell am I supposed to get out of this?

He'd hit the guy and knocked him down. He hadn't hung around to wait and see the outcome. Why did he come back? He must be really stupid. He could say it is a personal matter, not a police thing, see what they say. He was unhappy Tesanee had called for help though. She had no business asking them. He wouldn't hurt her, she must know that. They'd been together for ages and he'd not laid a finger on her before, but they had wound him up and had outnumbered him, so he'd struck out to protect himself.

He was disgusted with himself, fighting in a public place, a car park of all places. Look at the state of him, his best suit torn, and his leather shoes scuffed.

His mind was clear on this though, no more explaining, when he got out of this, he was off, and he was never coming back.

****

Toby drove and Al lay dozing with the seat back flattened as far as it would go.

"So much for your minding, what the hell am I going to tell Sonia when she sees my face."

"We'll tell her the truth when she gets back but for now, she doesn't need to know."

"We've got to get him back for this, I need to work out a plan."

"That's for tomorrow, tonight you need rest, in the morning we'll work out what to do. At least we know where he is tonight, he'll be out by tomorrow though and then we don't know where he'll go."

When they arrived home, Al was feeling nauseous and light-headed. Toby helped him into the house and suggested a long soak in a tepid bath with a chilled bottle of beer.

"You get in the bath and I'll bring you a beer and sort out the food. What do you want to eat?"

"I don't know there's not much in the fridge."

"Takeaway then, fancy pizza or curry, we could order."

"Pizza then, not curry we need to be moving around and I don't want to be caught short, get a meat feast or something you like."

"Okay while you're soaking, I'll phone and get it delivered. Got any takeaway menus?"

"There are a few in the kitchen drawer. My wallet is in my jacket pocket."

With both hot and cold taps running he added some of Sonia's muscle-relaxing Dead Sea bath salts. The smell of peppermint, rosemary and black pepper filled the air. When he was happy with the temperature, he lowered himself into the warm water. He had that wonderful feeling of tension relief, easing his aching body. He didn't appreciate how hard a car park road surface was until today. It felt like he was growing another head as well.

Toby found bottles of cold Pilsner in the fridge and brought one for Al.

"The nurse said not to drink alcohol with these painkillers."

"Ah get away it's not going to kill you and we're not going anywhere until tomorrow. I don't care who calls."

He went off and ordered two pizzas then called Jo.

"Hi Jo, how are you? it's been a hell of a day here so far."

"How's that? What have you two been up to?"

"I got here okay, we went to Alain's, had a spot of lunch and then we got a call to help one of his mates."

"Straight into it then."

So he told her about the fight. How he stopped it. The police arriving and the stitches on Al's cheek.

"You're alright though, are you?

"I'm fine, Al's a bit shaken up, that's all. They arrested the bloke. We're home and we're safe. I'll call you tomorrow night, bye love."

Al soaked until he heard the doorbell.

When they'd finished eating Al wanted to plan ahead. This was becoming personal.

****

Al woke feeling bruised and battered. He stood in the bathroom looking at his face in the mirror, his cheek and eye were swollen and turning a purple colour. The paper stitches were still on and it still stung like hell. At least he had no broken teeth. He was boiling angry and wanted to speak to Tesanee, *now*.

In the kitchen, Toby was sitting at the breakfast bar checking his phone. He'd made a pot of coffee and had drunk most of it.

Al walked in and said. "I seriously need to talk to Tesanee."

He wanted tea, so he put the kettle on to the boil.

Toby looked up.

"Morning to you too, how are you feeling?"

"Like I've just done three rounds with you."

"You'd look worse if you had, shouldn't play the hero, that's my job, you should have left him to me."

"Yes, where were you? I still can't believe he was so strong, he looked like a little runt."

"They usually are, you'd better persuade Sonia to stay another week, so the colour goes down before she gets back."

The kettle boiled, Al made tea then put bread in the toaster.

"We are going to see Tesanee this morning to talk to her about what happened yesterday. I don't care what she is doing or what Ash says, she needs to tell us why she met Karl and what the argument was about. I'll call Ashley as soon as I've had this and finished my shower."

"Alain are you sure you're up to this? You're a location expert for the movie industry. That's all make-believe, not real. You have never been good in a fight. At the moment you're full of anger and you're not channelling it in the right place."

"I'm not stopping now we have to finish what we started. I don't like Karl at all now and he's just made it personal."

"Okay if you're sure. I'll shower while you eat your breakfast."

Al sat and contemplated what to say to Tes, while he ate his toast and drank his tea. It had all happened in a rush, from Ashley calling to getting knocked out by Karl. He kept thinking back to the journey down when Ashley was telling them about Karl's temper.

Ashley told them about times when Karl would just lose it

and storm off in a huff or shout at his mum and say he was going to the pub. He said it was a bit weird because Karl was not a big drinker or a drunk. It's more like it embarrassed him when he couldn't get his own way, like a child with a temper. Maybe he needed anger management.

Toby had finished in the bathroom, so Al went to shower and clean his face up as best he could. When he was ready, he found Toby in the lounge watching the morning news.

"I'm calling Ash now."

"Right-oh, let me know when you're ready."

He went to the kitchen to a quieter area. Ash's phone rang four times before he picked up.

"Morning Alain, how are you today?"

He got straight to the point.

"Crap. I look like crap and I feel like crap, and I hurt like crap, listen, I want to talk with your mum, is she available this morning?"

"Well, I'll have to ask her but I'm sure she'll make time for you after what happened yesterday, I think."

"She'd better be, this job is getting serious, I didn't expect to be nearly hospitalised."

"Okay, I'll let her know you want to see her. I'll call you back, soon as." Ashley closed the call.

Al went back into the lounge where Toby was waiting "I said I would go to the police station and make a report this morning. So, we'd better go now before we see Tesanee."

"Do you *have* to go today can't they wait?"

"I think it's best don't you, get it out of the way. They will only be on to me if I delay it?"

"Let's find out what's happening to him."

"I don't fancy that bloody drive again."

"It's not so early today. I'll drive let's get it over with."

Five

Karl was in a dilemma. How to get out of this? It was so embarrassing to be in a cell overnight. He felt dirty, and he wanted to get clean then hide somewhere. He'd left the police station early, drove straight to the office flat, showered, and went to the office. Why did they call it a station anyway, no trains?

He was sitting at his desk trying to make his mind up. Eventually, he knew he had no choice he had to make the call. He answered immediately.

"Hello, nephew how are things with you?"

His mind was spinning. He couldn't get the words out. "Eh hello sorry to bother you, I'm in a mess. It's a big problem and I need to discuss it with somebody. Can I come and talk to you about it?"

"What is troubling you? Is it something bad?"

"It's Tesanee."

"What is wrong with her?"

He took a breath and calmed down "I would rather not talk about this over the phone. If you don't mind."

"Well, if it's that important I understand. Come when you can I will be waiting."

He rushed from his office immediately and hailed a taxi. As soon as he arrived, he was ushered into a side room to wait. His uncle came in a few minutes later and asked him what the problem was.

He blabbered out, "It's Tesanee she will find out about the money."

"What money?"

"She's planning on buying something she can't afford."

"You are not making much sense. Surely she will check her bank balance and when she realises she can't afford it she will not make the purchase Why is that worrying you?"

"That's not all. I left her last week, but I came back to explain. We had a big fight, she called two guys, and I had to defend myself. The police were called, and I was arrested. They have recorded it as a domestic problem, so they have let me go."

"You are a foolish boy. I thought you had changed."

"I'm so sorry I have messed up."

"Let me order tea, that will give you time to calm down and then you can tell me all about it."

His uncle dialled for green tea. He hated green tea, but it was a family ritual. They had to sit quietly until it had arrived and been poured.

"Okay go on with your story."

"The problem is when she checks the account. She thinks she has much more in there than there is."

"You are not making any sense. Are you telling me there's some missing?"

"Yes."

"Don't tell me you've taken it."

"Yes, and I can't put it back without her noticing. She will see the transaction."

His uncle thought for a minute. "Okay, I understand now. This has been happening over a period of time. You are worried she will realise what you have been doing and confront you."

"Exactly. now, what do I do."

"Sometimes we need to admit we have done wrong and confront the problem head-on but this time I think it is best if you leave. Go to my place, the one in the country, and wait for my call. I will let the housekeepers know you are coming. Let me see if I can do anything. Remember, you still owe me and I expect a return." He stood to show the meeting was over. "I'll be in touch."

"Thanks, I will repay you."

"You said that last time. Now go, go quickly."

****

Even the car knew the way by now. Same journey three days running. When they arrived, Toby parked in the number one visitor's space. A young policewoman showed them into a side room with a computer on a desk and three chairs. She asked Toby not to interrupt while she asked Al to explain what happened while she typed it into a crime sheet. Toby would be next. She turned and asked Al a few questions regarding Karl and his demeanour.

"I understand why you stopped him from hurting Ms Thompson the first time, but do you think you provoked him after he returned?"

"No, I don't."

"Why do you think he came back a second time?"

"He said he wanted to explain, but he never got the chance. The manager told him to go."

"How did you react, and what did you say to him?"

"I stood up, walked towards him and said *'What is it with you, can't you see you've hurt her, just go.'* Then he hit me."

"Did you say it aggressively?"

"I suppose so, we had just been fighting in the road in between two cars. I was angry."

She finished the statement, printed it and asked Al to sign it. Then it was Toby's turn. He repeated what Al had said almost word for word. Only changing the bit where Karl knocked Al out and telling how Karl had rushed out again and drove off. He signed his form, and they made to leave.

Al stopped and asked.

"What will happen to Mr Hurnston?"

"Nothing. He's not here we released him this morning. We have recorded it as a domestic assault."

"But we were in a public place not at home."

"It was between two people living together so it's domestic."

Al's pulse was rising. All he could think about was they will do nothing about this. "Not what he did it wasn't. I'm not living with him and he knocked me out"

"Calm down, please. We are gathering all the statements. Thanks for yours. That's it for today we will contact you if we need anything."

****

Al was seething as they arrived at the car.

"He's going to get away with it."

They got in and Toby turned to Al as he drove away, and said.

"Possibly, the police have too much on their plate to bother about a bundle in a McDonald's car park."

"Jesus Toby, he knocked me out. It's bordering on grievous bodily harm."

"Come on, let's go to see Tesanee. Maybe she can shed some light on this."

Just at that moment, Al's phone rang, it was Sonia.

"Hi, darling how's Spain? Are you relaxing?"

"I'm loving it, so is Jess. We had a delightful evening at Che' last night. How are you getting on, you're not too bored are you?

As if, he thought.

"No chance, there's always something to do."

"Are you in the car? You're not driving, are you?"

"Toby came over to babysit me while you're abroad. He's driving."

"Hilarious. When did they arrive, Jo never mentioned it?"

"Jo's not with him, he's on his own, and don't read anything into it, there's nothing wrong, Jo's fine. He's just spending time with me. Brotherly love you see. It doesn't happen often."

"Okay well if you're both all right then I'll call you in a couple of days."

"Give my love to Jess, I love you, bye."

"I love you too. Love to Toby."

He hung up, glanced at Toby.

"Sonia sends her love. I had to tell her you are with me because if Jo can't get in touch with you, she will call Sonia".

"I understand they are both suspicious women."

40

They were on M23 motorway and as they crossed over the M25 Al received a WhatsApp message. Al read it to Toby

"Ash says he's been going back through Karl's bank account. Last August he made quite a few payments for fuel and restaurant food in Coniston. They went out on or around the same time and he assumed something connected them, so he thought maybe, Karl had lived near Coniston for about a week."

"Coniston, that's in the Lake District, isn't it? I wonder if Tes knows about it."

"Maybe. The question is, could he be on his way there now?"

Al wasn't really concentrating; he was thinking of a way around the next phase without getting another black eye.

****

When they arrived at Tesanee's house she was waiting for them. Oh, my word thought Toby as they approached the house. Back home they would call this a mansion. How much money do these people have?

Al had known Tes for a long time so he knew she would always make tea before talking. This time was slightly different though. As they stepped into the hallway she looked at him. "Oh, Alain I'm so sorry, your face."

Al put on his best disarming look.

"It's nothing Tes. I've had a black eye before."

She turned to shake Toby's hand.

"Nice to meet you again, Toby isn't it. We were never formally introduced. Ashley told me you are brothers and I can see the resemblance. Please go into the front room while I make us a drink."

They went through to the lounge and waited while she prepared a fresh pot of tea. Although Toby preferred coffee he wasn't complaining today.

He had a look around and saw the photos of Alex and Ashley in fancy frames. "Jesus Al, you've got some rich mates."

When she came in Toby spoke first.

"It's a pleasure to help Tesanee. We're sorry about yesterday, it got out of hand."

She poured the tea then sat on the settee, curled her legs under her and said.

"I know. Karl was angry, and he took it out on you Alain. I'm sorry too. Does it hurt a lot?"

Toby listened quietly while he stirred his tea.

Al ignored her question. He wanted answers.

"Do you know where he is Tes?"

"No, Alain I don't, he was taken to the police station and I have no news of his whereabouts."

"We've just come from there and he's been released.

"You were at the police station. I didn't know they took you there."

"They didn't take us we went this morning to give statements. So, he never came here?"

"No, I hadn't seen him for a week until yesterday."

"Where has he been for a week and why did you agree to meet him there?"

"Firstly, I don't know where he's been. He called and wished to explain but didn't want Ashley around, so he suggested that place."

"It's a strange choice don't you think, so far away."

"I know, but I don't know why."

"Anyway, he's missing again. Ashley just sent a message about a place in the Lake District. Any ideas?"

"I've never been there. What place?"

"Ashley thinks he might own property up there."

"Well, he never mentioned it. How could he buy somewhere without my knowledge?" Suddenly tears welled up in her eyes. He waited while she took a breath. "Sorry."

"Don't be."

"Some people say everybody has secrets."

"I think everyone has at least one."

"You think you know someone then you find out there's a lot you don't know."

"We'll go after him and try to reason with him."

"Thank you, it's good of you to do this. If you need extra help, you know Decha. You might want to ask him. He knows many people who may help. I'll ask Ashley to call him and say you will pay him a visit."

"Decha! Yes I know him, I haven't spoken to him in years though. Do you think he's involved with all this?"

"He's been around. He was Alex's friend. He still visits Ashley. We all worked together once when Ashely was a child. Remember?"

"Yes, I do. Okay, we'll look him up. We won't bother you again unless we need to. We'll be in touch when we know anything."

"Thanks for the tea, Tesanee," Toby said.

Toby led the way out while Al gave Tesanee an extra-long hug, then whispered something in her ear "Keep it up we're sorting it out. It's going to be alright."

Toby couldn't make it out. He thought nothing of it as then they left her thinking about what would happen if they found Karl.

Al's mind was two steps in front already.

"Let's grab lunch, then we'll see Decha."

****

Al's face was stinging on the way home. Probably all that scowl-ing and smiling he thought. He was also thinking about the Lake District and could he ask another friend for help. When they arrived home, he asked Toby to drum up something to eat in the kitchen while he went into the lounge and called that old friend.

"Hello, Hannah here, how may I help you."

"Hi, Rocky it's Alain."

"Jesus! Where have *you* been, it's been so long, you don't call, you don't text, you don't email?"

"I know, I know, I've been busy."

"Busy, it's been twenty years."

"Come off it, it's the same for you." He paused before continuing "Look I'm sorry I don't blame you I should have kept in touch."

"I wish you had. To what do I owe the honour of this phone call?"

"I'm setting up something, or someone up, and I'd appreciate a little help."

"Well okay, I forgive you. I always had a soft spot for you. Someone you said. What are you looking to do?"

"Could you do a little scouting around for me? I'm looking for anything you can find out about a person named Karl Hurnston?"

"Why, what's he done?"

"Nothing to worry yourself about. I've lost him and I think he has been up your way recently, especially around Coniston. He could be returning. I need to find him."

"Can you spell that for me? There are variations?"

Al spelt it for her.

"Thanks, 'Karl Hurnston', okay I'll ask around. Can't promise much though if he's just an occasional visitor."

"Anything will do. All I can tell you is he's around your age, five-ten, Asian complexion and he's not short of a bob or two so he could have been splashing the cash as we say. Dresses smartly and oh he drives an expensive car."

"He sounds a right 'Jack-the-lad', okay I'll let you know as soon as I find out anything."

"Call me if you don't find anything too, please. If he's up there, I'll be coming up as well, so maybe see you soon. Thanks for helping Hannah."

"No problem it will be nice to catch up. Hope to see you too, bye."

Toby shouted from the kitchen "Have you finished yet, grub's up, it's time to eat."

Six

Toby parked in a street close to their nearest station, where they caught a train to central London. At Victoria station, they changed onto the Victoria underground line and caught a packed train to Oxford Circus.

When they came out at street level, the place was buzzing with shoppers and tourists. Crowds were on every street and every corner, crossing Oxford Street or Regent Street or waiting to cross.

No sense rushing so they checked the maps app on their phones which showed the quickest walking route to Golden Square. It looked easy enough. They strolled down Argyle Street past the London Palladium Theatre, showing the *Cinderella* pantomime, turned left onto Great Marlborough Street, right onto Carnaby Street, right onto Beak Street, left onto Upper John Street and left into Golden Square. A traditional London Square with lawns and statues. Entertainment companies and a couple of food outlets surrounded the square. Suddenly, Al had a tingling feeling down his back. At the end of the street, he stopped, turned, and looked back, almost without thinking.

"Look at that shoe."

In the centre of the square stood a huge statue of a stiletto-heeled shoe.

"Yes, Toby that's a famous statue, see the heel is like a knife or dagger."

"That's a new take on Stiletto Heels."

There was a raised central paved area, with a statue of George II on a plinth. One of only two in London.

The meeting wasn't until four o'clock so they had time to spare. After two hours of travelling, enough time to grab a drink. As they walked across the square Al spotted a Scandinavian Bakery, come coffee shop so he suggested they stop for a coffee.

Toby ordered two Americanos and a Danish pastry each then sat at a table by the front window, Al went to freshen up. Their suits were top-notch Saville Row, rented especially for the meeting. Cool silk, cotton blend material not too heavy for moving around quickly. Al always thought you need to feel and look good, to fit in and become what they want to see. He thought he looked like a world traveller but what he saw in the mirror was a scared rabbit. He was always anxious, it seemed, must be hereditary in his family.

He warned Toby as he sat at the table. "We have to be careful, you only get out what you put in."

"I know the rules; a smile goes a long way. Where's this bloke from again?"

"The Philippines, remember he doesn't know what we know and please look like my minder, they won't be expecting you to be anything different. Keep the watch on and recording at all times and remember names too. I'll do the talking ok."

He got a smug look from Toby.

****

Ten young men spotted Dansen and his partner at the cross-roads of Oxford Street and Regent Street. They immediately fanned out, watched and waited.

The ten youths, two on BMX bicycles, followed the pair from the station until they were near Golden Square. They watched them cross the square and go into a coffee shop, then one of them took out his phone and reported in.

"They have stopped at the coffee shop by the tattoo place. I can see one of them sitting near the window."

"Which one?"

"Person or coffee shop."

"Both."

"The Swedish place and I can see the big guy."

"Well done. Let me know when they are on the move again."

"Do you need us to keep following?"

"No, you have done enough. Keep watch though. I'll call you back when they are leaving."

****

Al's mind was whirring, at five minutes to four he said, "It's time to go." As they left the bakery he kept thinking of questions he wanted to ask.

The sign on the door would send most people away. It read 'Ten Tonne Tattoo Studio'.

Toby gave a confused look.

"A tattoo place, you sure this is right?"

"This is the address I was given, let's see."

They went in and the receptionist asked them to look at the design book while the tattooist finished tattooing a client.

Al wasn't messing around. "We don't want a tattoo we are here to see Mr Decha."

The tattooist looked up and pointed to the back wall of the store where two massive men in dark suits were lounging by a plain door, one on the right and one on the left. Al and Toby approached Toby on the left and Al on the right. Al introduced them.

"My name is Alain Dansen and this is Toby Dansen." Then for a second time, he said. "We are here to see Mr Decha."

The doorman on their right took a mobile phone from his pocket, it looked tiny in his massive hand, dialled someone and spoke softly in his own language. After the call, he nodded to the guy on his right.

"We have to pat you down."

"What you're joking we are friends of Mr Decha."

"I'm sorry my boss says we have to. It's not personal it's the procedure."

The size of these guys was slightly off-putting so Al and Toby raised their arms.

Mr Universe on the left checked Toby and the runner up on the right checked Al.

Mr Universe turned and punched a code into a console by the door, shielding it from view with his massive frame. The huge metal door slid to the left with a loud hissing sound. The two bodybuilders stood aside and ushered the Dansens into a corridor. Toby and Al stepped through into a dimly lit, air-conditioned hallway and were met by, what looked like the doormen's twin brothers, slightly smaller, but not by much. The door hissed closed behind them. There were two cameras, one over the door behind them positioned to look down the corridor and one looking straight at them from the other end of the hallway above another door.

They walked side by side towards the second door, glad of the air conditioning to cool them, one twin in front and one behind, no one spoke. There were no handles on the second door so the escort in front looked up into the camera and the door opened.

They stepped into a long rectangular room with low lighting and pale-yellow walls. There were scarlet coloured lounge seats covered with velvet and a pale grey carpet. The walls were adorned with paintings and the room smelt of cigar smoke. There had been loud conversations from about a dozen men but they quietened down and stared at the two men entering their space. The Dansens had formed a calm space in a vibrant place.

The men were all merry, whisky drinking men, smoking big fat Cuban cigars. It was like a scene from an old movie. Al sensed quickly that they were not at all welcome. He felt like they were breaking into a closed world.

He turned as he felt a hand on his shoulder. The hand belonged to an Asian man, half a foot shorter than Al and Al's not six feet tall. a round, weevil shaped man who had a big upper body, short legs and dainty feet.

"Mr Alain it is a pleasure to meet you again after so many years," said the man.

Al knew if he was to convince this man to help them, he had to gauge everyone in the room, each reaction. To read the room quickly watching facial expressions, eye movements and body language.

"Hello Decha," Al replied, "I'm sorry I never knew your other names."

"No matter, will you sit and take refreshment with me?"

"We've just had coffee."

"This is a bit stronger and I'm sure you'll like it." His tone was friendly, but he and his friends had hardened looks that were all business. "Is this your brother? He looks like a younger version of you. Although much larger."

Al remained standing but offered his hand which the Asian man shook firmly. He knew the man was just a year older than him, forty-six. He also knew he was adept at languages, fluent Arabic, perfect accent-less English, Thai, his own Cebuano, as well plus a few more.

Decha steered them to a table with three chairs. Toby was smiling to himself. Behind Decha's back, Al mouthed 'Don't say anything' as they sat down.

"This is Toby, Toby meet Decha," Toby towered over Decha, nodded, bent forwards and shook Decha's hand.

Toby looked down and thought, he reminds me of Bob Hoskins, short but stout and really strong.

"I remember you liked to drink whisky, Mr Alain? I have a few bottles of Brora 1972 they are forty-five years old now."

"It's a fine old whisky from Scotland."

"Did you know the Brora distillery was built as far back as 1819 by the Marquis of Stafford, although it was known as 'Clynelish' then, until the opening of the Clynelish Distillery in 1968, when they changed the name to 'Brora', it was a heavily peated whisky in those days which makes it so smooth."

"We would love to try a glass of your whisky, wouldn't we Toby?" Toby nodded.

A waiter brought the whisky in fine cut glass tumblers and refreshed Decha's glass. Al felt they were going up in the world.

"The release of the 1972 Brora forty-year-old in 2014 was the most expensive single malt ever released," Decha said after they all had tasted some,

"So you are a collector of fine things. I bet you have collected many things over the years, hidden away."

"A few, some too precious to show."

"I didn't know you were in England. The last time we met was in the Middle East."

"I have been here for around four years now. I like it. It is a great city and good for me and my business. What brings you here today?"

"Right! I'll come to the point. I see no other way but, to be frank with you."

"That's quite as it should be. One should avoid trouble for as long as possible."

"Anyway, as I said I will get straight to the point. The reason we're here is an old friend of ours; you remember Alex Thompson? Well his wife Tesanee thought you may be able to help us. She asked her son Ashley to call you and arrange a meeting. She gave me this address."

"Ah Ashley, he is a fine boy, also a friend of mine. He did call and asked me to help you. He said I knew you so I checked soon after he called. I remembered you from a long time ago. I'm always glad to help old friends, if I can, what is it you require?"

He's looking nervous thought, Toby. Twitching and looking at his drink.

"We're hoping you don't mind; we're interested to know if you know of a man named Karl Hurnston."

Decha looked up smiling. "The only Karl I know is living with Ashley's mother, Tesanee."

"Yes, that's him, we are trying to find out about his background."

"I don't know him I never saw him when I visited. That was a few years ago though. I only visit Ashley nowadays."

"Tesanee told us Karl arrived here from Singapore."

He's doing it again. Toby could see this man didn't like to be questioned.

"Is that so?"

"Yes. She said you know many people from the old days when we worked together. You might have heard of Karl. We think it's possible he changed his name from Malaysian or Thai to English. Is there a translation that would suit that name?"

"Karl, translated would be Karit."

"Is that a true translation?"

Decha looked thoughtful "Let me think." He took his time considering his answer. "Yes, it is. I do not know about Karl but there is a Karit who is a person of interest to me."

"Oh! why is that?"

Toby raised his arm to get a better picture, sipped his whisky and glanced around the room. Here he goes, this is getting uncomfortable for him. I can't wait to play this back.

"It's a personal matter. Karit borrowed a lot of money and has not returned it." He looked down into his drink and swirled it around while thinking before continuing. "I cannot say it's him. I only went there a few times. As I said it was years ago."

I knew it. He's hiding got something. You are doing great Al, keep him sweating.

"But it could be him."

"It is possible, yes, but he has been gone from my mind a long time now. I would like to find him though. What is your business with him, why do you want to know?"

Al ignored Decha's question for a minute. He wanted to see if Decha was more forthcoming with information or even if he was willing to help find Karl. So he asked another question of his own.

"If it's him, and I think it's a great possibility it is, can you help us. How do you know him?"

"Before I answer I would like to know why you want him? He steals things, has he stolen from you too?"

"If it's him, you know he's been living with Tesanee. You

know Alex died a couple of years before she met him and Karl kind of took his place. Now he's disappeared and so has most of her money."

"It seems we have a common problem Mr Alain, again what do you want from me?"

"We need your help to get her money back."

Al kept digging. In the back of his mind, he was thinking careful now. He repeated. "How do you know Karit?"

"I gave him his first job."

Toby looked straight at Decha. There it is, the first tell. He knows him alright.

"You gave him a job! What kind of job?"

"Collecting donations."

Al didn't ask what kind of donations and he didn't want to know either.

"So, what happened to make him run?"

This time Decha ignored the question. He was thinking aloud now. "In my country, we have to forget any quick judgements or prejudices we might have. There are so many factors involved but I always had a suspicion because he did not like the work. He always wanted the quick way to the top job, but it is our way to teach the young people to respect their elders and to work your way up."

He looked like he was in a daze. He was looking beyond the room like he was in another place for a minute.

Al brought him back to the room. "It is the same with us if you are learning a trade."

This was good information. I hope you're getting this Toby.

"Anyway, he's run from you and you're still trying to find him, is that so?"

"Yes, he has been gone for a long time but I have never forgotten about him." He looked away thinking. Al was hoping it wasn't that he was giving them too much.

Al took a drink and thought of his next question. Questions, questions, he couldn't let on too much.

"Don't get me wrong but in my experience, it's to do with his upbringing. It's in the past and If it is him, I would like to find out about his."

Al sipped his whisky to give him time to think.

It was all about power to Decha. The name Decha means power in his country. He would want to know everything Al and Toby knew, and he would want to find Karl or Karit, whatever name he used, before them. Therefore, Al had to choose his words carefully.

"Look, if he ran from you he must have had a reason and now he's run again, he obviously has problems with commitment. He's a thief and he's been getting away with it so far. We want to stop him and get Tesanee's money back. Will you help us?"

Decha leaned back and gave that some thought.

"That is all very well Mr Alain but why should I help you, I don't care about her little problem, he has a lot of my money and I will find him one day."

"Well, we think Karl is Karit and we may have an idea where he has gone and we have a plan on how to get all Tesanee's money back."

"What do you think Mr Toby."

"I'm only here as an observer so I have no opinion, I will do whatever Alain wants to do."

Great answer Al thought, good old Toby.

"Okay Mr Alain let us share, shall we?"

At last, they were getting somewhere.

Seven

"Fine, you first," Al said.

"You came to me for information, I want to see something in return first."

A bit of diplomacy was needed here.

"Okay well, we've already told you the name he's using now. He's been living with Tesanee for about eight years and has been slowly moving her money into his account."

"Ashley has not mentioned this or his mother, and now he's disappeared with it," said Decha.

"Yes, and you still haven't told me why he ran from you."

"I will continue. His father and my father had a disagreement, and he felt he couldn't carry on working for me."

"What was it about?"

"It was a private matter, and we dealt with it personally."

Decha had finished his drink, so he called for another and they all had a fresh glass.

While they were waiting, Decha stood up. "Will you excuse me I need to talk to my colleague for a minute?"

Al looked up at him. "Certainly."

When Decha had left Al turned to Toby and spoke quietly "What do you think Toby, it's not what I expected?"

Toby answered in a whisper. "I'm amazed at him telling us all this."

"We need as much as we can from him. He wants info from us so he can find him first. I'm not giving him that much."

Decha returned, sat down and after a sip of his whisky said. "Are you okay Mr Alain, Mr Toby, shall I continue?"

"We are fine thanks Decha. Please continue."

"Where was I?"

Decha looked pained as if remembering was hard for him.

"I'm so sorry for bringing this up I had no idea, I apologise if it upsets you."

"It is okay; it was a long time ago. Karit didn't show respect, and one day he did not show up for work. We tried to locate him, but he had disappeared. I haven't seen him since."

Another small sip, too much and Al would lose his tongue.

Decha continued. "Where was I, oh yes, he went missing. We searched for him in our country. Sent out people looking, asked informants, everyone we knew but nobody had any information. We decided he had travelled abroad, but we never knew where. After all, it is a big world, Mr Alain."

"Did you give up?"

"Never, but we slowed our efforts until I eventually saw no use in wasting time or money on him."

"You didn't come here looking for him then?"

"No, as I said, I have been here for a few years now and he has faded from my thoughts. I have got bigger things to occupy me nowadays."

"Okay well we will find him and when we do, he will regret he stole from anyone."

"What is all this about Mr Alain? Why do you care? I thought you were a location expert for a big motion picture company. Not a private detective."

"You did check me out didn't you. I keep busy with small projects. I am just helping a friend."

"I hope so, is that all."

A thought came into Al's mind and he chanced it.

"One more thing, do you own any property in the Lake District?"

Decha was physically shaken, he looked away to hide his face as he'd had the fright of his life but he quickly recovered. "I am afraid I don't."

"Well, that's it for now. Thank you for your time Decha.

We promise to contact you when we have found him. As I said, we only want to get Tesanee's money back and then you can have him. Just one last thing. What is Karit's family name?"

"It is Sunthorn, Mr Alain, Sunthorn."

Al looked pleased with himself. "I'm glad we got that sorted, and it's not even five o'clock yet."

As they left Decha picked up his phone and made a call.

"They are on their way out. Let them get a couple of roads away and then stop them. You know what I want, rough them up a bit, teach them a lesson, not too much mind, just enough to slow them down a bit."

"Yeah yeah! No problem, we'll make it look like a mugging."

****

They went back along the dark corridor and out onto the street.

Al wasn't convinced. "He's not giving much away. We didn't find out a lot, did we?"

Toby knew the kind of person Al was referring to. "He's a good poker player, he almost kept a straight face the whole time in there. He only lost it a couple of times."

"I think we got his interest though, don't you?"

"Yes, now we know he's looking for Karl too. He's not going to wait for us to contact him. He's going to watch our every move until we find Karl and try to take him before we can."

****

They were still chatting as the entered Beak Street. At first, someone just shoved past them. Al turned and glanced over his shoulder, almost without realising. Then a gang of youths turned and barred their way. A couple showed up behind on bikes. They huddled around Toby and Al.

Toby counted about nine or ten, all shorter than him. He

shouted at them. "Out of the way, lads. Let us through." The lads didn't move. "What's going on? What are you after?"

One of the group beckoned to him.

"Come here and I'll tell you, I won't hurt you I just want to explain something."

Al grabbed Toby's arm.

"Don't be silly Tobe, let's go."

"It's all right Al, I'll be fine."

As Toby approached, the lad said. "We want your wallets and phones; on second thoughts you can keep your fucking phones."

Suddenly he kicked out and caught Toby between the legs, right in the balls, he went down, clutching his crotch. The pain was agonising. As Toby tried to get up, Al ran, without thinking, to defend his brother.

"Leave him alone." Then he struck out with his right fist and caught the guy smack on the jaw. He slumped back into the arms of a stocky guy who grabbed him.

The two lads on bikes jumped off and grabbed Toby. They held him down, one on each arm while another grabbed his hair, tugged it back to make him watch what was coming. He grappled to burst free, then felt something pushing into his side.

"Don't fucking struggle or I will cut you, understand?"

He still tried to pull away but they were surprisingly strong.

Somebody pushed Al and knocked him onto the pavement. Suddenly the others were all over him. He immediately curled himself up into a ball and brought his arms up around his face. Some were beating his arms and back, others kicking his head, legs and ribs. He moaned and groaned as Toby struggled with his captors.

"Easy now, easy." Said the one with the knife.

He needed to save Al, but they continued on kicking until a group of sightseers came dashing to their rescue.

"Get away from them you thugs." A tall well-built man with an American accent cried out. One of his friends began calling for help.

One of the gang called out "Stop, leave him. Go."

They pushed Toby to the ground and had one last kick at Al. then the thugs scattered. Running off leaving Al in a heap by the kerb.

"Bastards. Are you okay fella?" A woman asked.

Al sat up and leaned his back against a wall to clear his head, his ears were throbbing, and his ribs ached.

Toby came across to help him up and shook the man's hand "Thanks for saving him."

"This is not the type of sightseeing we came to London for," replied a tall American guy.

"It's not always like this." Then Toby looked at Al.

"Your ear is bleeding. You need a doctor."

"I'll be all right. Come on, let's get out of here. At least we've still got our wallets." To the Americans he said. "Thank you all for helping, enjoy London."

****

Toby put his arm around his brother's waist, and they weaved their way past shoppers to the station at Oxford Circus. He thought they were safe now. It didn't last long though. As they went down the stairs, he saw some of the gang waiting for them in the ticket hall. He helped Al past them towards the Victoria line escalators. The gang spread out, mingling with other commuters. A couple followed them down onto the platform. He kept urging Al, who was shuffling along, to move quickly, fearful for them, wanting to catch any available train. He saw the platform, southbound at least he thought.

A couple of the gang arrived with them and called to the rest to hurry. The crowded platform made it difficult to hurry. A train arrived, and he prayed the doors would open near them. Luck was in, but as they pushed their way onto the train, he felt Al pull away and a hand in the middle of his back, push him onto the carriage. Someone inside gripped his arm to hold him from getting off. Looking back two of the gang were holding onto Al, stopping him from getting on. The doors closed, he was on the inside, facing out, at his brother being held by the two cyclists who had held him.

As the train drew away, he felt sick not knowing what would happen to Al.

He had to think about what to do. He wasn't sure where he was going. There was no phone signal in the tunnels, but he knew he had to get off at the next stop and go back to find Al. All he could hope for was the gang hadn't hurt him again.

When he arrived at Green Park station, he crossed to the northbound platform and waited for the next train. He didn't know they had left him at the station and that Al planned to catch him up.

When the train arrived back at Oxford Circus, he pushed his way off apologising and dashed across to the southbound platform to search for Al. There were so many passengers it was impossible. He hoped he was still on the platform and the gang hadn't taken him with them. He let a train leave then looked up and down the platform. He thought he recognised someone sitting near the far end. Could it be him? His suit looked crumpled but the right colour. He called out

"Al are you ok? Don't take the next train wait for me."

The man didn't respond. More people were arriving, so he moved up towards him. It had to be him. A train was pulling in and the crowd were moving. His heart reached out to him.

Please wait for me. Please wait.

****

Al went to step on the train, but he felt a hand on his collar pull him back. Arms circled his neck and a hand on each of his arms. He felt weak from the kicking and had no strength left for more fight. People were boarding the train and saw him fall back but ignored him, needing to get on. He looked up and saw Toby on the train. Standing next to him he thought he recognised one of the guys from the gang who had been kicking him holding

Toby by the arm. Once the train had left the station there were just six gang members and himself on the platform, two were holding him.

The biggest one faced him. "Remember, I asked you for your wallet."

Al ached all over, but he had a resolve about him. A few more aches wouldn't make a lot of difference.

With a croaky voice, he answered. "Yeh well, you can't bloody well have it."

"What did you say? Speak up we can't fucking hear you can we guys?"

Deep down he found inner strength and shouted: "I said you can't have it."

"Then I'll have to take it, won't I."

Al braced himself for the punch.

The big mouth punched him so hard in the stomach it knocked the wind out of him. He tried to bend forward but strong arms held him upright.

Strangers saved him again. Passengers this time. A crowd arrived on the platform and looked up towards where Al was being held. The guy who threw the punch decided enough was enough and waved them away.

"Let's go, there are too many witnesses here now. We've separated them and slowed them down a bit."

They left him leaning against the wall. He looked around, disoriented, saw a bench. He just needed to rest awhile. He wasn't sure where Toby was, so he sat and waited for the next train, blood trickling down his neck, from his ear.

There were hundreds of people on the platform, surrounding him. He let a couple of trains go before standing up and moving along the platform. It was less congested, and he wanted to board at the front. He heard someone shouting somewhere to his left on the platform, but there were so many people he couldn't see who it was. His head was spinning, and he felt so tired. I've got to get on the train and find Toby is all he could think. I need to clear my head and look for him. He was sure one of the gang had got on with Toby and was holding him. A train was pulling in and the crowd were moving. The shout came again, and he looked down the platform and saw Toby jumping to try to see above the crowds. He relaxed and sat back down to wait. Another train full of passengers left and then Toby was there He sat down next to him.

"Jesus let me get you home, I'm so sorry I should have listened to you."

"It's not your fault, you couldn't know that was going to happen."

"I'm not much of a minder, am I?"

"Stop that, it's all right, let's get out of here I need another bath, whisky this time. No painkillers and no beer."

Eight

The big mouth made a call as soon as they were on the street.

"We left the one called Al at the tube station. We separated them. The big one called 'Tobe' went on without him. We hurt the small one, he won't be going anywhere soon. We certainly slowed him down a bit. He needs maybe a couple of days to recover."

"Okay well done. I'll make sure it's worth your while. Come and see me tomorrow."

"We made it look like a mugging gone wrong. Too many people about to hang around though, and don't worry they won't link us to you."

"Good. I'll be in touch."

He hung up and they separated to become invisible. They would meet up later.

****

When Al and Toby got home, Al took another soak in the tub. He poured muscle-easing bath salts in this time.

Toby made hot drinks and came to sit on the toilet seat to talk.

"We can't keep this up I've only been here one day, and we've been in two fights already. You look a complete mess. My god, you're stronger than I thought. I put a wee dram in yours, every little helps. Sonia had better stay another couple of weeks. She sent a text while you were in the bath, I took the liberty of answering, saying you were okay and hoped she was having a nice time. You look like you've been in a car crash. Just saying."

"Yeh, you said that already, it feels like it. It's not that so much, just a few bruises. Thanks for answering Sonia she would have called if I hadn't answered. What about the suits? We have to return them tomorrow."

"We'll call Neil tomorrow morning and he can do it. He's not doing much else. I'm sure he can explain."

"You're right he's pretty good at talking himself out of trouble."

He went through into the lounge to wait.

When Al surfaced Toby had poured more drinks and ordered a takeaway.

"I ordered a curry, I can't eat pizza two nights on the trot. Now settle down you need to rest and recover from that beating."

The house phone rang. It was Ashley, Al put it on speaker. Ashley was shouting "He's just bought petrol on the M6 motorway."

Al was speechless, Toby said. "Where Ashley?"

"In a service station near Lancaster between Junction 32 and Junction 33."

Al looked at Toby and said. "He's on his way–"

Toby finished for him "To the Lake District…"

The bed felt soft after a car park, a pavement and an underground station platform. The cut on his ear looked worse than it was. Toby had cleaned it up and covered the small cut with a plaster. At first, he found it difficult to find a comfortable position without pain in his limbs or his ribs. He had overworked his mind, and something wouldn't come to him. Eventually, sleep came. He was so tired and dosed up with painkillers he had a dreamless night. When he woke up after two minutes, seven hours had miraculously passed.

The weather had taken a turn for the worse during the night, so they spent the morning taking stock and planning. Al phoned British Airways to check availability. He wanted to go after Karl.

"The only flight I can get is lunchtime to Manchester."

After calling Neil to arrange returning the suits Al asked Toby to check the watch video.

"I asked him to buy us breakfast as we're crap at food shopping."

"We haven't had time. Too busy out fighting for our lives. Neil is a nice bloke. You must be good mates."

"He's lonely, he just wants something to do. He'll be enjoying this. Let's see what we missed yesterday."

They sat at the breakfast bar. Toby removed the memory card from his watch, plugged it into Al's laptop computer then started the home movie.

Al pointed at the screen. "There's Decha and the waiter."

"He looks like he could break your neck if he wanted."

"Decha would I'm sure."

"I mean the waiter."

"Yes, the room was full of tough-looking men, every one of them capable of handling themselves in a brawl. Did you notice how quiet it was after we arrived? They were scrutinising us."

"Watch Decha's body language, he's blinking and somewhat twitching every couple of minutes. Fiddling with his bracelet, looking away from you. It's as if he's making it up as he talks."

"That's interesting I hadn't picked up on that while we were there, I was too busy working out what to ask him. I thought he'd had a few too many drinks."

"Typical of someone hiding something. Look at his eyes, the pupils dilated the first time you mention Karl."

"How do you know this stuff?"

"Joanne and I work with people who have mental problems. A few of them make things up most the time. They pretend to be someone else, so they tell lies. They train us to spot this type of thing."

"I can't believe he didn't make the connection to Karl."

"That was when he stopped to consider it. Then he said he didn't know him."

"Surely he hadn't changed that much, older perhaps."

"Remember, he said he hadn't seen him. We don't know how Karit looked though, do we? Before he left home, I mean. He could have completely changed his appearance, hair colour, contact lenses."

"He probably dresses differently I'm sure. Now he can afford too."

"Well, we need to put him back where he belongs then, don't we?"

"We will, look here he goes to talk to his mate."

"Yes, he was only away a few minutes, so it couldn't have been much. Do you reckon he's telling the truth about the family problems?"

"Well, I'm sure It happened. Why would he lie about family involvement?"

"I know what you mean. It's an amazing thing to admit to."

Al's mobile phone disturbed them. He looked at the screen and answered the call.

"Hi, Hannah how are you getting on?"

"Hi Al, I've found out something about your mystery man."

"Great. What is it?"

"He's definitely been up here, and I can confirm it was last summer. He may have been more though."

"Okay, where did he stay?"

"I can't say where he stayed, but he was definitely in the Leven River Hotel for dinner and drinks."

"How did you find that out?"

"I asked around my circle of friends. Old mates, I've known for years. Well, no luck at first but then, I couldn't believe it. The word must have got out. I got a call from an old friend, you remember Eleanor, she was part of the crowd. We always went out every weekend. She used to be one of my best mates back in the day, we were always together. Anyway, she says someone resembling that description bought her a drink in there one night. So I went there, and the barman remembers him but he's sure he wasn't staying there."

"That's amazing, well done, I remember Eleanor, how is she?"

"She's okay but divorced and lonely now, no kids, so she goes out a lot."

"You all used to go out a lot whether you were married or not. Anyway, I'm coming up today, so I'll be in touch when I get there."

"Today that's great, how are you getting here?"

"BA to Manchester then we'll drive."

"Can't wait. Call me when you're settled, and I'll come and find you. See you later."

Toby was listening, but he only got Al's side of the call. "Who's Hannah?"

"An old friend from way back, she lives in Ulverston near Coniston, I asked her to ask around. Oh, and I remembered something else in my sleep. Decha said Karit's name was Sunthorn."

Toby wasn't listening, so he said. "So, we're going up there. Might as well I suppose. What was that his name, yes I remember."

"It's an anagram."

"An anagram of what?"

"Hurnston is an anagram of Sunthorn."

"Christ almighty, so it is, you're so bloody clever sometimes. So, he changed his name using the straight translation from Karit and an anagram of his surname. Did you get Decha's surname? I remember you saying you never knew his other names when we arrived yesterday."

"No, good point bruv, I must ask Tes."

"It's interesting though. Decha likes fine things, and he's also a collector. It all sounds expensive too. It might help us. Anyway, he knows who we are after and he's searching as well. If Karl or Karit or whoever he's called owes him a lot of money, we will use that when we find him. Give back Tesanee's money or we tell Decha where to find him."

"That's not bad, but there's another way too."

"I'm sure we could torture him, but I don't want you in any more fights. Let's find an easy way."

"I have thought of a much easier way."

Neil came for the suits and dropped off a bag of groceries.

"Jesus Christ Al, you said you were all right. Well, you don't look it, pal, look at the state of you. Are there any wounds I can't see?"

Al was looking ashamed. "I'm okay it's just a few bruises."

"I meant mental ones. You need to be careful or you'll finish up in hospital. Here, this is what you ordered, eggs, bacon, beans, mushrooms and tomatoes. I couldn't think of anything else."

"What no sausages?" Asked Toby.

"You don't want much, do you? You owe me a tenner. Where are the suits?"

Al was more forgiving. "Thanks, Neil. Do your best with the suits, we're sorry we've messed them up."

On his way out he called back. "No problem. I'll call you later."

Al stared at Toby sheepishly "Don't look at me like that. Come on, create your magic in the kitchen. Let's have brunch."

While Toby created a breakfast come-lunch with a mixture of what Neil had brought, Al made a few calls.

After, he went into the kitchen; the smell was heartwarming. Toby was preparing some kind of Irish omelette.

"I've just recalled something else. One of those thugs said something before they took off."

Toby glanced up from cutting tomatoes "What?"

"He ordered his mates to leave and then he added, 'We are only supposed to slow them down a bit'. Or something like that."

"What! Are you sure, they shook you up? You could have imagined it."

"I'm certain. It means they were waiting for us to leave Decha's place."

"Do you think he arranged it? It could have been when he talked to his mate."

"This changes things. I'm not sure how yet. Let's eat."

While eating, Al was still pondering about yesterday.

"I want to check out the video again. This time the whole way through."

"There's a lot to look at I forgot to switch it off until we were on the train home."

"Are you saying you might have footage of the gang?"

"Suppose so. It might not be any good though. My wrist was everywhere during the struggling."

Toby fast forwarded until they left the tattoo shop. The picture wasn't perfect, but they caught a glimpse of the lads on bikes and a couple of the others as they gathered around them. Then they held Toby's hands down by his side.

Al was annoyed now. "I was hoping to see the boy who punched me."

****

After Toby's best omelette, Al said. "Let's go back to see Tesanee I have a few questions about Decha."

She ushered them into the lounge again. "What can I do for you now. I thought it was over."

"Tell us about Decha. You knew him well, didn't you?"

"I did, a long time ago. He comes from a dangerous area and his family were tangled up with some criminal people."

"Do you mean it was gang-related?"

"It's a sensitive subject but his sister's brother-in-law was imprisoned for a gambling fraud."

Toby coughed and cleared his throat.

Al stopped, his train of thought scrambled. "You're joking."

"I don't joke about family matters Alain. His older sister Raylai married a man called Kawee. Kawee has an older brother called Kunchai. Kunchai was put in prison."

"That's a lot of K's."

"Anyway, her father-in-law and her father had a disagreement."

"About him going to prison."

"Yes."

"Did his father disown her father-in-law?"

"It was like disowning, but in our country, it was more banishing them, his sister included."

"Is Kunchai still in prison?"

"No, he served four years, but he's been out for the last five years now."

"Did Decha see his sister while her Kunchai was in prison?"

"He saw her, but he had to keep it a secret from his father, he would have been unhappy with him if he knew."

"May I ask what the fraud was about."

"It was a strange one. Do you remember the English football match-fixing at the end of 1997?"

Toby's eyes went up, he sat up sharply, and nearly choked on his drink. "I can't believe this; you're telling me they were involved in that."

"They were heavily involved, Toby, and he was caught. Not all the syndicate were found, and a few got away."

Toby chocked out "A security guard informed on them I seem to remember."

"You're right Toby he did, or they would have continued and made a fortune."

"Many of them did I bet."

"I heard they celebrated a six-figure payout. Still, gambling is the biggest sport in our country, alongside basketball. People can place money on 'spot bets' which predict the outcome of the minutiae of a game."

"Well, it's hard to believe. Thanks for telling us, Tess. It might help with our search. That's it, for now, we'll be in touch."

They went out, Toby was still shaking his head.

"Unbelievable, absolutely unbelievable. You couldn't make this up."

Nine

They drove straight home threw a few things in backpacks and drove to Heathrow Airport.

During the drive, Toby was thinking about Decha and Tesanee and the morning's visit. "I nearly choked when she told us about Decha's brother-in-law. It's hard to believe he was involved in that football fraud. Remind me about it again."

"I can remember most of it. I think they fixed four games, but I only remember the first three. One at Upton Park where West Ham played Palace, one at Selhurst Park where Wimbledon played Arsenal and one at The Valley where Charlton played Liverpool.

"The lights had gone out with the scores level. The ref abandoned each match, and they had paid millions of punters out on the draw. The police caught them when a security guard called the police at the third attempt."

A band of rain, sleet and snow were moving south over the Midlands, East Anglia and the south-east. It was snowing in Cheshire, and it was very windy everywhere. As usual for any British airport in bad weather, they delayed the flight. Heathrow is not different, the public-address system announced there was ice on one wing, so the ground crew would spray it to help thaw it out.

Eventually, after around forty-five minutes wait in the departure lounge Al and Toby could board. The plane was an A319-100, one of the smallest in the British Airways fleet and it was full. They had just taken their seats towards the back of the plane; the air stewards were checking the seatbelts when a small amount of smoke came from around the overhead lockers a few rows up from them. A few passengers towards the front panicked and a couple wanted to get off. The air stewards tried their best, but they wouldn't be pacified so the cabin crew allowed them to leave. It was looking like a nightmare day as this meant waiting for them to take their luggage off.

While this was being sorted out, they ushered everybody off the plane and back to the departure lounge to wait. An air steward told them that those people had transferred from another flight and had spent most of the day trying to get home, they didn't want to chance any more mishaps so had elected to catch a later flight. This was another setback for them.

Toby was furious "I didn't believe all this Friday the 13th business but there seems to be something going on."

"It's ridiculous to think like that," Al told him, "it'll be okay when we get going."

"I hate internal flights at the best of times, small planes, no leg room, I told you we should drive. It would have been less stressful."

"Not on our roads, there's so much traffic, you'll be fine, it's only an hour's flight to Manchester, we'll get a car there, just sit back and relax maybe get forty winks in before we arrive."

It had been Toby's idea to call Ash back last night. They asked him if his program could trace Karl's bank transactions to see if he had a place he might run to. Ash had searched and called back with two places. None looked likely to be in the Lake District. Al was hoping the rental car would be all right.

The delay cost about an hour but no big deal. What could they do anyway? Around forty minutes into the flight, the pilot announced for the crew to prepare for landing. The weather had worsened during the flight the rain was lashing down and it seemed like they were in for a tricky landing. Al was reading the inflight magazine when he turned to Toby to show him a piece about Hong Kong.

"I've never been to Hong Kong; I wouldn't mind going, how about you?"

Toby was shaking, and his voice was higher than usual. "How can you be so calm we are in big trouble on this plane and you don't seem to know?" Not shouting, but he was tense.

"Toby, Toby, Toby keep your voice down, I can't do anything about it can I."

"You could at least show you care."

"I trust the pilot to know how to land this thing and if not, the airport will help him out."

Just when they were descending the pilot pulled up sharply as a crosswind hit them.

"Jesus!! I told you we're in a mess."

Al didn't know how but he'd always had a knack of slowing his heartbeat, so he could remain calm.

"I thought you would be my minder not the other way around, hold on and stop fretting the pilot knows what he's doing."

They landed at the second attempt in atrocious rainfall. The plane stopped a short distance away from the terminal, so the stewards ushered them onto buses to get to the arrival's hall.

Toby needed to feel his feet on the ground, get inside the terminal and calm down.

"Can we get a coffee and a bite to eat I'm famished, and I need the caffeine?"

"The food's a good idea but maybe a decaf for me I'm wired as it is."

There was no need for customs, so they were through in no time. They had arrived in Terminal 3, so they found Costa Coffee. Al had a one-shot and a Danish pastry, Toby had a double shot and a bacon roll for his nerves.

The queue at the rental car office was another thing though. After queuing for half an hour, the salesman told them there were no mid-size group cars left. Toby was ready to argue but Al told him to drop it and see what they offered. He offered an upgrade to a new Automatic Volvo V40 Inscription, very stylish.

The offer pleased Al. "Well, this is a turn up for the books."

Toby couldn't believe it "Unbelievable, this never happens."

"Do you want to drive?"

"I can't wait. At least I can drive it with the seat in a comfortable position. Hey, here's a good one I heard recently. Which car is the same forwards and backwards?"

"No Idea."

"A racecar, get it, race car, it's spelt the same both ways, forwards and backwards."

"Ha bloody ha, now drive will you."

"You're cheerful."

"I'm tired and everything aches, also too many early mornings in one week."

After entering their B&B address into the maps app on Toby's phone they set off. Ash knew the address and had shared all the phones with the find my phone app. They had made a WhatsApp group too. The drive took them west out of Manchester airport, which is in Cheshire county, along the M56 motorway then a north turn, onto the M6 motorway into the county of Lancashire past small villages with workmanlike names like Locking Stumps, past small towns with exotic names like Cinnamon Brow, past the M58 turn off to Liverpool and skirted the city of Preston towards the Lake District. As they approached Lancaster and Morecambe Bay, Al asked Toby to dive into the seaside town of Morecambe.

"What on earth for, it's inhospitable as a winter resort you know, and I haven't brought my swimming shorts."

"I need to get two sim cards for the cameras."

"Jesus, I thought you were all organised."

"I never had time to replace the ones in the cameras yesterday after the attack we went straight home."

Al had hurriedly packed his cameras and wasn't sure if the memory cards were empty or not, but he always liked to have spares.

Toby was thinking I'd better keep him talking or he'll fall asleep. Al stifled a yawn.

"You've been up here before, haven't you?"

"A few times. Last time was nearly twenty years ago, I came up once a month for nearly a year, site surveys for documentaries about the oil rigs. Sonia is from here."

"Really? I never knew where she came from. Do you still know anybody here?"

"A couple, I'll look them up while we're here."

After picking up the memory cards they detoured along the seafront past Jack's Shack, The Beach Diner Bar and the arcades, all closed for the winter, some closed forever by the looks. Then they picked up the A6 for Cumbria.

"Good job you know the way then. Where's the next turning we seem to go a long way north?"

"Watch out for Charley Island then turn left onto the A590, it's windy but keep on it until we get to the A5092 towards Lowick Green. It's like a big u-bend. towards Barrow-In-Furness, local folk say it's a big cul-de-sac, one road in and the same road out."

Continuing towards their bed-and-breakfast near Coniston Water, both quiet, thinking, until Al said.

"You know Coniston is the second biggest lake in the Lake District after Windermere."

"Okay, mister know-it-all, tell me about Ash's dad."

"Well, I remember him being a big guy when we first met then I saw him lose a load of weight. We did a trade show together once and were staying at the same hotel. One morning I was waiting in reception and he didn't show so I called his room, but I couldn't rouse him. Eventually, I got the manager to open his room door, and he looked in a real mess.

"He wasn't going to the show that day, for sure. We'd had a few drinks before turning in the night before and he told me he'd had a sugar overload. He drank non-alcohol beer after that."

"Urh! that's a shame, that stuff is awful, it leaves an aftertaste and no alcohol."

"Well needs must. Before he died he'd looked weary and it wasn't because of excessive exercise. He was into martial arts, he was a black belt in aikido, so he had to be strong to throw people about, but he didn't do other exercises, he sat at a desk all day, he didn't go running or anything like that."

"It's hard dieting and training at the same time maybe he stopped going the aikido to get control of his weight."

"I know Tesanee was checking everything he ate or drank when he was at home."

"What about when he was out and about?"

"I think he was good; he knew the risks. It was about twenty years ago when Alex had called me and asked if we needed any help. I'd known him for a couple of years, and he'd worked for me before, so I agreed to take him on. Alex had joined, and he'd been an integral part of producing our internet package that had been an innovation.

"He'd needed the job to get his wife and son a visa. Tesanee was from Singapore and so was their son Ashley. He had arranged visas for them both, so they could live in England with him. They rented a flat near our office."

"So, he was a good mate of yours then?"

"For a few years, then he died, suddenly."

"Not expected then?"

"No."

"Come on Al, you already helped them once, how many times are you going to do this?"

"Let's see where it takes us, he's paying, anyway."

They were nearing the lakes now. Loads of small villages with old names dotted along the way. Toby was checking the road signs, "Well that's Great."

Al turned to him. "What is?"

"You missed it."

"Missed what?"

"That village."

"What are you on about?"

"That village we just passed was called Great."

"Really? Well, there are some very old named places around here."

"Yes, and a load of country bumpkins."

The continued on, past Stockbird Head and Tottlebank Coppice. There were plenty of bridges, they passed Newby Bridge, Penny Bridge, Spark Bridge.

Their sat nav showed around a one-hour forty-five-minute drive but they had added forty-five to it with the detour. It was approaching nine o'clock by now and the low clouds covered the fields in smoky blue candy floss.

Al gazed out over the cloudy fields and saw lights from buildings glowing through the mist as they came upon the Shepherds Inn.

The place looked old, as if from the Middle Ages, with oak beams and low ceilings. They went to the check-in desk and the registered. The receptionist asked them to wait while she called the manager. He arrived and apologised because he had made a mistake with the bookings and they could only stay one night. Toby was at the end of his tether and about to blow his top when Al sent him through to the bar while he finished checking them in. it was annoying though, as they couldn't tell how long it would take them to find Karl. They would need to arrange alternative accommodation for tomorrow and any further nights.

Before the receptionist could check them in, she wanted a credit card. Thankfully, Al had an empty bank account, well almost empty it had ten pounds in it, especially for these kinds of moments. They could pay cash when they checked out. After checking in he dropped their coats and bags in their rooms and found Toby at the bar with a pint of local bitter. It was a free house and well stocked with all makes of beer and whisky, so they were spoilt for choice. Toby was partial to a blended whisky whereas Al found a single malt to his liking. Toby looked pasty.

"Thanks for driving, are you all right?"

"No, I bashed my head on a bloody beam in the doorway."

That's why Al called him his little big brother, he's nine years younger but half a foot taller.

"You've got another bump on her head, don't forget to duck, I'll buy you a drink, do you want a 'Jim' it will kill the pain?"

"I will need a few, it's low here. How did you find this place, and do you know there's not even an en suite, we have to share a bathroom down the hall?"

"Stop moaning, I found it on the internet and it's perfect for us to keep under the radar, for now anyway."

"Under the radar, under the roof beams you mean, the ceilings are so low, I'll stick with beer tonight, whisky gives me a sore head and I've already got one, I'll find a seat, order me some food while you're there."

Al ordered pub grub at the bar. While the barman recorded his order, he looked at himself in the mirror behind the bar. He took in his bruised face and sore ear, maybe he had taken on too much. Then he turned and looked for Toby and found him sitting at a table in a corner, right by a big log fire. There was a black and white spotty dog dozing by it. He looked weird with one black ear sticking up and the other white one flopping down over his eye.

"I've ordered you steak and kidney pudding with mash."

Toby took a swig of beer. "Good man, that's one of my favourites."

"I'm having beef and Guinness pie."

After eating and settled with another pint of beer, Al's phone buzzed, it was Ashley.

"Hi, Ash, what's up?"

"I got a ping from the tracking software. Karl has used his credit card at a hotel close to yours."

"Blimey that was quick we've only just arrived an hour ago."

"Yes, it's working really well, he's at the Leven River Hotel, I looked it up, it's a swanky beauty spa in a place called Newby Bridge looks about ten minutes from you."

"Yes, it's not too far we passed it, we're in Lowick Green. If he's just checked in, he's not going anywhere tonight, we'll look around tomorrow, thanks for that, is everything all right with you?"

"All okay thanks I'll be in touch if anything else comes up," and he closed the call.

Al relayed what Ash had discovered to Toby, and they planned the next day.

"That's the place Hannah told us about, isn't it?"

"Yes, it seems he likes it there."

Toby had been quiet during the meal but now he stood up to get more drinks. "Firstly, we need another hotel tomorrow as they're full here."

"Yes, we'd better plan to stay a few days just in case, I'll change the return flight."

"Know anywhere close by?"

Al pulled out his phone and started the maps app.

"There's a few around here but he's back towards the motorway and he could be away quickly, so It's better to move closer to him. Get us another drink and I'll call someone I know."

Toby went to the bar to get more drinks and Al called Hannah. She answered after four rings.

"Hello Alain, where are you."

"I'm at the Shepherds Inn and I need some local help can we meet?"

"Straight to the point, no change there then, I don't know Alain I've been thinking it's been a long time and I've got a family now."

"I'm sure you have but I need local knowledge to help a friend. Come on, Rocky I need your help."

"Please call me Hannah, I left that name in the past."

"Sorry Hannah, can you help?"

"Ok but don't come anywhere near me. I'll come to you, but not now, is tomorrow morning all right?"

"I don't know where you are but thanks, see you in the morning."

Toby came back and asked, "who was that?"

"Hannah, she's coming over in the morning."

"I can't wait to meet her."

"Yes, she's a lovely woman who I met while I was living up here."

"She must know somewhere we could stay, come on drink up let's turn in I've had enough for one day and I don't want to be late for breakfast."

A sudden weariness came over Al as he climbed the stairs. He needed to recharge his batteries. He could have done with another long soak, but the thought of searching for the bathroom put him off.

"Mind your head. You don't want another bump, or you'll look like Shrek, or worse, like me," he called out as he went into his room.

"Funny Ha-Ha!" Al heard as he closed his door, he could still feel the bump at the back of his own head.

The room was nothing special, a double bed, a chair, a wardrobe, a bedside table with one drawer containing the usual Gideon's Bible, a reading lamp and phone. He'd just open his bag to get his sleep shorts when it rang. It was Toby.

"Last one of the day. What question can you never truthfully answer yes to?"

"No idea."

"Are you asleep?"

"Goodnight Toby."

Ten

He undressed quickly, throwing his clothes onto the chair, and flopped into bed, his mind was still active though, but he needed to sleep. He'd thought about what he would say during the journey up. About how he knew Karl was stealing her money. About how Karl was shifting small amounts into his offshore bank accounts. It ran through Al's mind as he lay in bed.

He'd even toyed with the idea of confronting him about Ashley's theory but decided to keep it for another time. It was still a theory after all until they could prove otherwise.

As he relaxed on the soft bed, he became aware of the damage to his body. All the bruises and cuts he'd suffered in the last few days ached. They slowly came to the surface. He'd been so busy he had pushed them to the back of his mind. He thought of his own parents, nothing like the hardship of Tesanee's. Still, they had had little money to keep them all fed and clothed. His father worked hard from dawn till dusk to support them all. His mother fretted and broke down more than once. This was getting overwhelming. He hadn't planned for any of this.

He checked his smartphone apps and all his gadgets were working ok. Then he closed everything down including himself. The sheets felt so good, soft smooth cotton, probably brand new, with a warm quilt. He decided to buy a new set when Sonia returned.

****

Karl woke suddenly, with a feeling of breathlessness, panicking at the thought of an intruder in the room. Sitting up, he looked around seeing no one. The sound of seagulls outside and the wind buffeting the window panes calmed him. He had been dreaming and was unsure how long he had slept. He guessed it was 4 or 5 am. In his restlessness, he had thrown the covers off during the night and the bed was cold. He hated the cold. Warm weather was one of the things he still missed from home. He associated English winters with snow and freezing temperatures, painful fingers and toes. He pulled the covers over him and settled back down, thinking it would be warm in his home country now. He dozed off again for a couple more hours, then rose with the early morning sunshine, showered and went in search of breakfast.

The housekeepers, Mark and Alison, were nice and looked after him whenever he came to stay. He took to eating in the kitchen with them. They didn't get many guests, so they were glad of the company. He ordered coffee and poached eggs and thought about his next step. He knew he had to talk to Tes, knew he had to explain his actions. How could he explain though? She would want to know where the money was. The money he had stolen. There was no explanation or reason behind why he had taken it, other than he had wanted the money. It was an obsession of his.

He'd run before and managed to stay hidden for a few years. Got himself a good job at a finance company He thought he was safe until they had found him. He'd been drinking in a bar with work colleagues when one of his old mates had spotted him. His trouble was he'd become complacent, forgotten to keep low, enjoying himself. That was seven years ago. He'd had a troublesome life until then, he'd never had much growing up. His father seemed to do all right though, but he shared nothing with him or his mother, he was always away somewhere or another. He didn't really know him. When they had caught him, he had lied, saying he didn't have their money any more. He told them he'd spent it. They wouldn't listen, they threatened him, made him fear for his life, so he'd agreed to work for them again. This time spying on Tesanee.

A friend of his uncle's had sponsored him to come to England. They had rented a place for him close to her, arranged a job transfer to a finance company in London, in the city. It was scary at first. A strange country with no friends to help him settle in.

They sent a guy over for a weekend to show him who she was. He gave him a list of things they wanted, including who she worked with, who she socialised with, how she lived her life. Most importantly, they wanted to know how Ashley was, his schooling and his favourite things. All about both really.

So, he followed her and found out she worked as a cook in a pub kitchen. He drank and ate in the pub where she worked and watched her come and go for a while. He chatted to the barman about her and found out she had recently lost her husband; she was lonely and vulnerable, so he made a move to get close. He praised her food and flattered her looks, all the while reporting back. He offered to take her to dinner; she declined a few times. It took a few weeks but eventually; she agreed. He didn't force the issue he wined and dined her until she trusted him. After six months he moved in with her. Her son Ashley never trusted him though, most probably thought he was taking her away. It was never his intention to stay this long, but he had become contented. He wasn't in love but finally, he was happy for the first time in his life.

In the beginning, he had made regular reports back but gradually the reports became further apart until they had stopped altogether. Then one day four years ago, his uncle had called him to say he was coming to see him. He had arranged a meeting in the city near his office. Karl never knew the reason behind this facade, but he was getting paid to report back and he had not done so for months.

His uncle arrived to find out why. Karl knew his uncle was a dangerous man, so he was afraid to see him, but he had to. His uncle reminded him of his duty to repay his debt. Karl thought he'd done enough over the last seven years, but his uncle showed made him this would never be the case. He'd never be free even if he could raise the money. There would always be *'interest'* as his uncle put it.

Tes had not welcomed his uncle, and he had never seen him at the house. Ashley had remembered him though. They had known each other from back in the Philippines. When Tes mentioned an old friend had arrived Karl had pretended not to know him. Playing along with the game.

He had stolen from her now, owed them both, so he hid it. This time he would not get caught.

On the other hand, Tess could have found a way out for him. That stamp must be worth a fortune. If he had it, he could offer it in exchange for his freedom. Then they might release him from his promise and let him go his own way. He couldn't let his uncle know though. Not until he had it. If he found out he would get it for himself.

The guest house was off the beaten track. His uncle had only bought the place as an investment. His plan was to do it up and sell it on. So, until it was finished, there wasn't a lot to do, and he was the only guest. He had found the hotel a few miles away was great for meeting people, and as it was a spa, he could swim and relax as well.

Before he went out, he decided he would need his hat and gloves today.

****

Al woke up to a ringing sound with three thoughts in mind. What time is it, where am I, and why? He looked at the bed-side table and saw his travel alarm clock was doing its job. He silenced it with a slap on the alarm bell. Eight o'clock, so there was the first answer. The second came to him slowly after he closed his eyes to sneak a further couple of minutes under the covers. An old coaching inn in the lake district, Karl Hurnston, where are you? was the third.

The weather had brightened the following morning, with misty fields outside as Al went in search of the breakfast room. Toby had already found it and he'd ordered coffee and was perusing the menu.

"Hi Tobe, how did you sleep?"

"Out like a light. You?"

"Like a log. I haven't slept like that for a long time. You could always sleep anywhere."

Al was thinking logs are much better, they don't move much.

"When I'm tired, I don't have a problem. I got up early so I could use the bathroom without queuing. Bloody water is soft up here, I had trouble getting dry after my shower. Did you know it's the only thing that dries as it gets wet?"

"What is?"

"A towel."

"You're full of them aren't you."

Hannah arrived just as the waitress came to take their order. She put her head around the door and smiled. She was wearing a powder blue fleece pullover, against the winter chill and she looked happy to see him. Her hair was fashionably short with light-coloured highlights. Even in her forties, she was still a beautiful woman. Al beckoned her in to join them at their table. She came over and they hugged gently, remembering. She kissed him softly on the cheek.

"Hi, Rocky."

"I asked you not to call me that, what the hell happened to your face?"

"Sorry, it's how I remember you," He introduced her to Toby, "Toby, Hannah, Hannah, Toby."

"Hi Hannah," Toby waved.

"Hello, Toby, my god Al you look like twins, albeit little and large."

"Thanks for coming, was it a problem getting away?"

"Not really, I usually go shopping on a Saturday morning, so a small detour is not going to matter, what's up?"

"Have you eaten we're just about to order breakfast?"

"Just coffee please I'll have a latte with skimmed milk."

"You look good Hannah, dieting?"

"No, just can't stand full-fat stuff nowadays, must be an age thing. What's going on?"

"We're stuck for accommodation for a few days, these guys have double booked." Al noticed Toby was staring and kicked him under the table. "Aren't we Toby?"

A waitress came to take their order. Al and Toby ordered a full English breakfast each. Tea for Al, black coffee for Toby and Hannah's latte.

Hannah looked thoughtful "That's annoying. When did you book it?"

"Yesterday, it was short notice. We got here last night, not long before I called you."

"So, you're here looking for your mystery man. Have you found him yet?"

"No, we're still searching."

"Why is it a secret?"

"It's better you don't know."

Toby stopped staring and said, "We know where he is, but we are just monitoring his movements for now."

"He must be close if you're here."

"We think he checked into the Leven River last night," Al said.

"That's down by Newby Bridge."

"We know; is there somewhere close, so we can follow if he moves."

"Why don't you move there too, then you could watch his movements, mostly anyway."

"He knows us, and we're not supposed to be around here."

"You've got previous with him then by the look of you."

Toby laughed "He has, I always look like this."

"I can't think of anywhere close enough maybe you can disguise yourselves. How do you know he's there?"

"Never mind that we just do," Al said.

"There's always The Lakeview, it's a guest house in Blawith

close to Coniston Water. It's a bit run-down, I'm not even sure it's still open, but it's only about two minutes from here."

Al found it using a maps website, it looked secluded with a view of the lake.

"That's further away from him, okay I've decided we're going to the Leven River."

"Right! so how do you propose we do that, without being seen?" said Toby.

"I can sort you out something if you want?" Hannah offered.

"How?" Toby asked.

"Never you mind, I've got to go but I'll be back, you've got my number if you need to move quickly text me," she said.

"Thanks, Hannah we don't envisage going anywhere today," Al said.

Their food arrived, so they stopped talking to eat and drink. Al looked at Hannah, she sensed him staring so she finished her coffee, then rose, smoothed her dress, and messed with her hair. She hesitated as if to add something. "I'll call you." Then she turned and left.

Toby put down his fork, took a drink of coffee then said. "Why do you call her Rocky?"

"It's from the Rocky films, she used to have dark hair and wear a big full-length fur coat when I knew her. We used to hum the soundtrack, duh, duh duh duh. It's a long time ago now, she's changed."

They finished their breakfast then went to pack and check out. They didn't plan to leave yet though. After packing their stuff, they met up in the small lounge area by the bar.

Toby was getting impatient. "Call Ash and see if Karl's still there."

Al called Ash. Four rings again.

"Hi Ash, any news?"

"No, there's no more banking transactions since yesterday."

"So, in theory, he's still there."

"Seems so, I can't find out how long he's staying though, sorry."

"We've decided to move there. Our place has double-booked for tonight."

"Jesus, did you book it? You should have checked before you arrived. You'd better be careful he might see you, then he'll know we're on to him and then he'll wonder how we found him."

"Hey, calm down, don't get stressed. It's all under control we've got it covered."

"Well, if you're sure, I'll let you know if he checks out, that's if he didn't pay in advance or paid cash."

They closed the call and Al called Toby over.

"Toby let's go."

"You said we're not going anywhere soon."

"I'll call Ash and Hannah if we need them."

Al drove this time. He pulled out, and he turned back the way they had come, past penny bridge, past Stockbird Head, past Great to Newby Bridge to the Leven River hotel. To find Karl.

Eleven

Two young girls were playing classical music in the lounge at the Leven River Spa Hotel. One violinist and one playing the cello. They were from Vienna and they called themselves the Reflection Duo.

Karl was sitting close by reading the daily newspaper until it was time to leave. As usual, the world was a mess. Acid attacks, corrupt presidential campaigns, shares tumbling.

The sound was mesmerising as they glided their bows over the strings. It reminded him of his time in the youth choir. He'd been a member of his local church bible study class. He'd become a leader at his church youth club where he used to organise outings for the children and arrange evening entertainment on a Sunday after church service. Now he didn't want to entertain anyone, he was a multimillionaire running away to find a hiding place.

There were a few people to hide from not least Tesanee who he'd been fleecing for a while now and he'd taken a lot of her money. It had taken him a long time to do it. A little at a time so as not to show up too soon. He'd wanted it all and time to get away. She hadn't known. She was always working. She didn't have to, but she didn't know any different. Her family were hard workers, they had little or no money and their proud upbringing taught them working was the only way to survive. All she knew was she would never have to worry about money again, there would always be enough in the bank, forever. It was left to her from her husband's company when he'd died, and the company had been sold. Her son was shrewd, but he hadn't a clue either. He'd done it without either of them knowing. Time's up though, she will soon find out when she tries to buy that stupid stamp.

She'd want to know where the money had gone. Well, there's a lot to do to prove he's got it. Still, no need to worry now he's left, and it'll be virtually impossible to find him. He'd had to improvise quickly, bring his plans forward, go a bit earlier than he'd wanted.

At last, he felt free. It had taken courage, or at least he thought so, to have the integrity to raise another man's child as though it was his own. Now he was glad to be away. Defensive planning was a habit of his that would never die. He thought he was good at leaving no trace of himself. He would tuck himself away and become invisible. He needed to take time out and think about the next phase of his long-term plan. A plan that was still a long way from being finished but he looked forward to owning something special. Somewhere people would appreciate his tastes and give him a tidy income.

He read the financial section, deciding today he had no head for investments. It was always about the money. Just the thought of it resting in his bank account gave him a thrill. He always wanted more though, up till now. Now it was time to disappear again and it would cost him. He'd been patient with his uncle but now time was up.

That stamp though, Tesanee couldn't afford it but he could, and he knew exactly where to get it.

****

When they arrived at the hotel Toby checked them in while Al went to the garden and called Hannah. It rang a few times before she answered.

"What now, I'm trying to buy something to sort out your face, so you don't look so obviously like a gangster."

"Oh sorry, just wanted to tell you we have checked in to the Leven River."

"What the! Give me strength, I hope you're wearing a hat and dark glasses." She took a breath and thought for a minute. "Okay come and find me. There's a café at the Lakeland motor museum called Café de Bac you'll pass it on the way I'll meet you there. I've still got a few things to do this morning so give me an hour."

Al smiled "I didn't know you cared, see you there." and closed the call.

He found Toby in reception. "Could you take our bags to the rooms I'm going to meet Hannah? She's at the café we passed on the way here, back at the motor museum."

"Sure, give her my love, not literally. I'll have a look around while you're away. See you later. Call me if you need me."

Al drove back to find Hannah. He had plenty of time but wanted a half hour to reflect on the current situation. So, he drove slowly and enjoyed the landscape and thought about all that had happened.

He arrived and parked near the entrance. He was full of tea and coffee, but it wouldn't hurt to have more. He ordered a pot of tea and sat at a table by the front of the café to watch for her. He got his half an hour before she arrived.

When she came up to the table he stood and even though his ribs ached, he welcomed her with a hug. "I'm really grateful for your help with this, Hannah."

"Good, it's short notice you know."

"Sorry. I've ordered tea I hope that's okay."

"That's fine, it's great to see you. I often thought about you through the years."

She poured the tea and sat back to look at Al. "You haven't changed much. I still can't believe it has taken you so long to call me."

"Again, I'm sorry I wasn't planning on upsetting your life again."

"You're not upsetting anything. I don't have a man who I kowtow to anymore. I can't stay long though, but I'd like to see you again."

"Sonia might have something to say about that. I'm sorry to hear you're on your own. Is it you and the girls now then?"

"Just one left now. One has flown the nest. Single for five years. We manage okay."

"Are you busy later? We could meet you somewhere if you like?"

"How about later this evening, I always go out on Saturday nights with girlfriends, but I can make excuses to them."

"That would be lovely, but Toby is here and three's a crowd."

"We need to speak to Eleanor, so I'll call her and invite her. She'll be happy to make a foursome."

"That is a lovely idea it will be great to get a break from this."

"Yea this is weird. Here I've brought foundation, for your face, to help cover the bruising around your eye, and transparent plasters for your ear. It won't make the bruises completely disappear, but it will help. Here are two packets of ibuprofen are you in pain anywhere else?"

"You wouldn't believe where it hurts."

"I can guess where you want me to look. There's hair dye as well if you want it."

"That's going far but thanks I'll take it back to the hotel and show Toby."

"He's just like you but younger, and bigger."

"Yes, there are nine years between us."

"So, you're looking for someone who has ended up on my doorstep. This is a large area of natural beauty but has only a few towns. We usually get walkers or hikers not flash blokes with designer shoes and expensive cars. He's got to stay somewhere, and I have asked a few people who are passing it around. I'm sure we will find something. If he doesn't know he's being followed, then he won't be hiding. I take it he doesn't."

"Exactly my thinking."

"Can't you let me know anything else, it will definitely help."

"The only thing that's important is to locate him. Then we can decide what we will do about him."

"Sounds ominous. Are you going to hurt him? It's not like you to be spiteful."

"Look, I can't say too much but he's been stealing money, and they have tasked me to get it back."

"Jesus! how do you plan to do that?"

"We need to find him first then decide. Toby thinks he will pay it back if we ask him to, but I don't think it will be that easy. It's a lot of money. You'd better go, and I need to get back to rescue Toby."

They finished their tea and Hannah said sorry she had to leave. She didn't want to explain why she had been away so long. They arranged to meet later at the Shepherds Inn for dinner. Al stood and hugged her again before she left him there wondering.

*****

Toby grabbed a free newspaper from reception and went in search of Karl. His first thought was the gymnasium or spa. He found the breakfast room, the bar and the lounge, all empty at this time of day. The lounge had floor to ceiling glass windows on the back wall showing the garden and patios. The grounds were indeed beautiful, and the early frost was steaming in the sunshine.

He found the spa and the indoor pool housed in a glass-covered extension. They had added it after a refurbishment a few years earlier. There were relaxation beds around the pool where a few guests were lounging, reading, trying the daily trivia quiz or Sudoku puzzles, a couple were swimming. There were a group of people gathered by the windows playing Bag'O. A game with small bean bags thrown through a hole in a board.

The pool had underwater lights and even a weird crane contraption; he assumed for lifting disabled people in and out of the pool. There were two jacuzzis by the entrance and even a small bar serving soft drinks in plastic glasses. A sign by the door showed they kept the temperature at a constant twenty-two degrees, keeping the snowy conditions outside at bay. There was no sign of Karl though. Where the hell can he be, he thought. He must be in his room or out driving.

Toby didn't have swimming gear, so he took a seat away from the pool by the entrance. He was deep into the sports section of the newspaper when the lady on the next seat turned and spoke to him.

"Are you here on vacation?"

Taken by surprise he flustered his answer "Eh, no I'm only touring around the lakes. Just stopped for the weekend."

"Same here, we're on a walking holiday. This is our base hotel. We go out every day walking."

"I'm only here for a couple of days at the most. Just passing through and stopped off for a rest. You said 'we'."

"Yes, my granddaughter is with me. She's the one swimming breaststroke. I'm treating her because she graduated from university last year. This is a late Christmas break. I'm Steph by the way."

He tried to guess her accent, but it was a mixture.

"Toby." He offered his hand, and they shook. "Where are you from? I can't place your accent."

"Originally from Nottingham but I'm always travelling so I have lost my accent."

"A woman of the world. Do you still work?"

"No, I've not worked for years. I was a news correspondent, so I've worked in a few countries in my time."

His phone chirped, it was Al. "I apologise; I should turn this off for the weekend but it's my brother. We are travelling together; he's looking for me. Will you excuse me?"

"Of course, I hope to see you around the hotel. Maybe later?"

"Goodbye, I have to go. Nice talking to you."

Al went back to the Leven River. He couldn't find Toby, so he phoned him. They met in the lobby. and he explained he was going to his room for a rest. He needed to recuperate from the past couple of days and his body was hurting. When he got there he checked his messages, then surfed the internet, then dozed on the bed for a couple of hours. A guilty feeling passed over Toby, so he went to the lounge and called Joanne.

"Hi darling, how are you?"

"Hi Toby, I was wondering the same thing. I'm okay, missing you, that's all. How is Alain? What have you both been up to, it's all very secretive?"

"No, it's not, we are helping one of his friends to find someone. He's taken something and we are trying to get it back for him."

"Sounds exciting, are you both okay, you're not in any danger, are you?"

He hated lying but a little white lie wouldn't hurt. "We are both all right. We are getting close and I hope it will all be over tomorrow. I'm booked on a flight home on Tuesday. Plus, Sonia is back then too."

"I should call her. I haven't spoken to her for ages."

"Don't go calling her Jo. She's in Spain. She's back soon, call her when she gets home."

"You're right I should wait. Well, be careful and hurry home, I'll pick you up at the airport."

"Bye love."

A woman sat on a barstool at the end of the bar, close to a mirrored wall. She sat up straight holding a glass with her right hand and typed a message into her phone with her left.

There were a few empty seats, but Toby leaned on the bar at the other end and called the barman over.

"Good evening sir what can I get you?"

"I'll have a Hendrick's gin with elderflower tonic, plenty of ice and a slice of cucumber."

"No problem, sir."

While the barman made the drink, Toby asked. "Excuse me, do you know who that lady is at the end of the bar?"

"Are you staying here, sir?"

"Yes, I'm in Room 88."

"That's Eleanor. She's in here most nights."

"Is she on her own tonight?"

"It looks like it, although she could be waiting for someone."

"Oh! is he a guest here too?"

"I said could be sir, although she was with a man in here last night. I don't think he a guest, but he's been in before. I saw them talking last night."

"Did they stay at the bar?"

"Hey what is this, are you a detective or something. What's with the hat?"

"Yeah, I'm something, I'm just looking for someone."

"Well, he isn't here. Now here's your drink and you can continue looking?"

"Charge it to my room, will you?"

"That was Room 88. I didn't say it was a man, sir."

Another man arrived at the bar and the barman went to serve him. He came back soon after.

"Just so you know they went out as soon as they finished their drinks."

"Thanks."

Toby took his drink to a table in the lounge where he could see the door and Eleanor.

A short while later Al strolled in and joined him. He glanced at the woman then sat down. A waiter came to serve him. "Can I get you a drink, sir?"

"Yes. What local beer do you have?"

"Windermere Pale Ale from Hawkshead is the best around. It's won awards for the area."

"Okay, I'll have a pint please."

Toby glanced his way and complimented him.

"Going local, that's noble of you. I must say, you look rather cool in those dark glasses and that quiff."

"It's not much, but I had to think of something. I didn't bring much in the way of disguises with me. I can't see very well without my usual glasses. Hannah gave me this face makeup and hair dye, but I think that's over the top. I stuck a new plaster on my ear though."

"The barman says that is Eleanor at the bar. She could be waiting for Karl. She was here with a guy last night, but he wasn't staying here. I'm not convinced we're going to find him this quickly though. Too much of a coincidence."

"I think she's waiting for you, actually. Hannah said she was calling her to make up a foursome for dinner tonight."

Toby swirled his Gin and said. "Come off it Al. I'm the hired help, not a dinner companion. What will Jo say if she finds out?"

"She's not going to find out. If she does, I'll explain we're on business and we need information. Eleanor has some for us."

"I'd rather wait and see if Karl turns up."

"Sorry, I'm not leaving you here on your own. I'm also not going out with Hannah and Eleanor on my own. Let's take tonight off from chasing him and enjoy the lovely company. He doesn't know he's being chased so he won't be hiding, we'll start again tomorrow."

"I reckon we confront him and see what he does."

"Okay but only if he recognises us."

"I'm confused. I thought Ashley hired us to find him for Tesanee and now we have."

"Ashley says he was here. He may not be anymore. You're right we need to find him. Then we need to get her money back. I'm sure he won't give it back that easily though."

"Well, we can only ask him then see how he reacts."

"So, you think if we catch him and just ask him to pay her back and that will be the end. Somehow I don't think it will happen like that."

"Well, all this running around and chasing about is getting us nowhere unless we can speak to him."

Al went to the bar to speak to Eleanor. The barman saw him coming and signalled to Toby. He acknowledged with a thumbs up that he knew.

Al sat at the bar next to her. "Hi Eleanor, how are you? Hannah said you wouldn't mind going out for dinner with my brother and me tonight. With Hannah of course."

"Hello, Alain, nice to see you again. I would love to. I thought that was you over there staring at me. He does look like you, just a bit younger. I hardly recognise you, what happened to your face?"

"It's a long story and one to discuss over dinner."

"I haven't seen you for a long time. It will be nice to catch up after all this time."

"Okay, lets' go. Sorry, we are not dressed for the occasion we didn't expect to be going out with such classy ladies."

"You look okay to me. So that's your brother over there? He looks like you. Are you wearing makeup your face looks weird?"

"Hannah bought me some face cream to cover a bruise. I was in a fight and I took a hit in the face."

"Let's go to your room I will sort it out. You're not very good at putting it on."

"As long as that's okay with you."

Al went to tell Toby, and they went to his room. Where Eleanor reapplied the foundation and the bags under his eyes almost disappeared. He thought he looked ten years younger and felt a million dollars better. They went down to the lounge and Al introduced Eleanor to Toby. Then the three of them went out in the frozen night to find Hannah at the Shepherds Inn.

Twelve

The evening had turned cold quickly as it always did in England in January. All three of them walked in, shook off their coats and put them on a coat rack by the door. Hannah was sitting in the corner by the fire. Eleanor went to her first, and they kissed each other's cheeks. Al went to the restaurant reception desk to check their reservation. A waitress came and escorted them to a table for four in the low-lit room. Eleanor and Hannah were of the same age, therefore, Toby felt like a stranger amongst them, being much younger. He wasn't the best at small talk and felt uncomfortable at first, even embarrassed, until they ordered their food and the conversation settled down to find Karl.

Al broke the ice by asking Eleanor how she had been since they last met. "I remember when we were all out at that dance club in Ulverston. Those were great nights."

"We've been there a lot over the years, haven't we Hannah?"

"Yes, too many times to count."

Toby asked the girls. "Did you have a crowd of friends in those days?"

"We always went out together on the weekends. There were ten of us from school or college. We were a team. Weren't we Hannah?"

"Yes, our other halves were in some pub somewhere drinking and we were always dancing."

"So nowadays it's all changed for the two of you," Toby said.

"Massively." Said Hannah. "I have brought up two kids and Eleanor has worked as an air steward for most of her working life."

"Now I'm back on land and divorced. So is Hannah, but she has her youngest still with her at least."

Their first course arrived and their wine so they toasted old times and tucked in. Al wanted to pick Eleanor's brain and find out if she had, in fact, met Karl. So he brought up the subject after they had finished their first course.

"Eleanor, Hannah said you might have met a person we are interested in.

"She asked me and I'm sure I have. From her description anyway."

"Toby has a photo of him on his watch."

"On his watch? That's weird."

"It's a video recording watch. Like a smartphone but on a watch face. Show her Toby."

Using the button on the side he found the video and fast forwarded it to the fight in the restaurant. Eleanor's eyes were wide as she saw Karl punch Al.

"Yes, that's him. I can't believe what Hannah told me about him. My goodness it's a small world, isn't it? I can see how you got that black eye now."

Al gave Hannah a stern look as if to say 'You shouldn't have said anything.'

She looked across and saw his look.

"What, I haven't told her much. I was just trying to find out if she knew him."

Al blushed and apologised. "I'm sorry, I know. What was he like Eleanor? Tell us about him."

She took a drink to steady herself, then she told them.

"I met him last summer at the Leven River hotel, in the bar. I go there a lot now I'm on my own. The men are usually passing through. I can't stand the local guys anymore. All that air travel and big cities can do that to you. He was charming and bought me drinks. He was a smart dresser and extremely flattering. I remember his chat up line was so old it made me smile and it obviously worked."

She took a drink and thought more about it. The others waited while she took her time.

"I remember he had this beautiful looking watch, rose gold it was. He kept looking at it as if to show it off. I asked him if it was worth a lot and he said it was some French thing that was pretty unique, Jaeger something or other.

"We talked a lot that night and he took me to dinner. He didn't seem bothered about money. Paid for champagne with the food. I liked him and if he had wanted, I could have stayed with him but like I said most men are only here a few days if that."

Hannah was totally engrossed by now. "What did you talk about?"

"Everything really, as I remember. He was newly single, I was divorced so we were both looking for company and we kind of clicked."

"Was he staying here?" Toby asked.

"No, he was at the Lakeview up in Blawith."

"You mentioned that Hannah."

"I know. I wasn't sure if it was open though."

A sudden thought came to Eleanor and she added. "He said it's only open for special bookings and it costs a fortune."

"Obviously he can afford it," Hannah said.

Eleanor continued. "He took me there. It's lovely, they've done it up since you were here Al."

"I don't remember it at all."

"It was just a house back then. Now they've converted the barns to bedrooms. There's two each side of the main house and a couple of rooms in each."

The main courses arrived, and they ate quietly. Until Toby summarised. "So at least we have proof he's been here and he could be back. We need to find him."

Eleanor confirmed it. "Oh he's definitely been here and if I see him again I'll let you know."

They continued their meal with chit-chat, small talk and plenty of wine, all except Al who was still taking painkillers and had to drive. Toby and Eleanor enjoyed themselves and were secretly glad Al had suggested it. When they had finished, they promised to speak tomorrow. Al ordered Hannah and Eleanor a cab to take them home. They all hugged in turn and Al could smell Hannah's perfume. It was Poison by Christian Dior, he remembered it from all those years before. When she wore her hair long, dressed younger and more sexily. She had matured into a very stylish forty-year-old divorcee. He caught a glimpse of her black lace bra and wondered if she had matching underwear.

Eleanor wasn't ready to go home yet though. She suggested to Hannah they go to Sidings nightclub in Ulverston. Hannah said she would come for one drink then she had to get home. Her daughter was old enough to look after herself but she hated leaving her at home during the night.

Toby wasn't ready for bed yet either and wanted to investigate more. "Come on, let's go to find the house by the Lake."

Together with the wind and rain, Al also had to deal with a narrow road, full of twists and turns. There were no streetlights, so he had the headlights on full beam most of the way in case they missed the turning. Flicking them on and off as cars went by on the other side of the road.

According to Hannah, they would pass a farm on their left just at a bend in the road before it straightened out. Carry on for about a quarter of a mile and Lakeview was hidden behind a screen of trees and hedges. She said they had to be on the lookout for a sharp left turn.

She thought it was a five-minute drive, but the weather turned it into ten. They drove past small holdings and a few cottages. The hedges were above head height on both sides of the road. After half a dozen bends they saw the farm lights. Then there was a break in the trees to their left through which they saw the house. Al slowed, indicated left and turned off the road onto a large, half-circle, wrap around drive driveway, covered in gravel. He parked to the left of the main house beside a detached double garage.

There were four buildings that they could see. The main building, they assumed, was the owner's house. It was on a small hill that overlooked Lake Coniston. The outside walls were painted white with the windowsills picked out in maroon. There were tall columns on either side of an oak front door. It looked like an old American courthouse from South Carolina. There were no other cars parked outside but maybe there were a couple in the garage.

The garages interested Toby so he said, "You go and see if anyone's home, I'll take a look around."

It was drizzling, so he put a cap on against the rain and to aid as a disguise. He waited by the car while Al went to ring the bell at the front door. He walked over to the garages and after a quick look around, seeing no one he pushed against one of the doors. To his surprise, it wasn't locked and when it opened, he stepped inside. A light came on behind him, he turned and saw it was from a motion-activated light above the main door. Al had activated it as he approached. This made him think of CCTV but he hadn't noticed any cameras yet.

He closed the garage door behind himself, found a light switch on the right wall and turned it on, light filled the two bays. One was empty but the other one was occupied with a car covered by a tarpaulin, he pulled it off and was surprised to find an old, ice blue, Opel Monza under it. The bonnet felt cold to his touch. The walls adorned with tools and after a quick look around he found but nothing else of interest. He turned off the light, went outside and skirted the side wall to the back of the house.

There were two detached outbuildings flanking a raised garden. From the look of them, they used to be the barns Eleanor had mentioned. Now they had been converted to living areas. This is nice he thought. It must be worth well over a million pounds, possibly one and a half. They must have added eight extra bedrooms to the property. Two up and two down in each. It could pass as an expensive bed-and-breakfast or a small hotel. Minimum three or four bedrooms in the main house.

The back of the house was in total darkness and surrounded by trees, obviously planted for privacy and to keep unwanted visitors out. As he crept around the back corner of the house, he passed a window, the curtains were drawn across but leaving a small gap, allowing him to peer through. He saw a games room with a snooker table and a card table. He walked further along and spotted a set of patio doors. The curtains were open, so he went as close as he thought safe to the glass and saw what looked like a dining room.

He froze suddenly and ducked to the side when a light came on flooding out revealing a patio area. Karl came striding over to look outside. Toby thought he was about to be discovered. Karl was standing inside looking directly at him. He stood as still as possible not to call attention to himself. Then he realised Karl couldn't see him. He was using the glass as a mirror to comb his hair and brush fluff from the shoulders of his jacket. Toby assumed he was getting ready to go out, and the light inside had made the outside darker. When Karl turned, he moved away from the doors out of view and flattened himself against the adjoining wall.

His heart was pounding and his breath coming fast, he leaned forward with his hands on his knees. The rain was stopping his breath from being seen. He was glad of the silence so he cursed under his breath when Al called out.

"Toby where are you, there's no answer at the door."

He waved to silence Al, as he came around the corner and joined him at the back wall. He pointed at the patio doors but the light had gone out. It was dark and he saw no one.

Al mouthed "What's up?"

They were talking in whispers "I saw Karl in the dining room."

"Jesus. How?"

"I came round from the garage, saw the curtains were open so I looked in, then the light came on and I saw him getting ready to go out."

"Are you crazy? Did he see you?"

"No, the light inside made the glass dark, so he couldn't see me. It's a trick of the light, see. He was using it as a mirror, smartening his hair and brushing his jacket. It gave me a fright though."

"You think he's going out?"

"Yes," Toby was still breathing hard but calming down gradually. "Did you try the door? It might be open, the garage was. Nobody out here though it's all quiet, no automatic lights either."

"No, I didn't try it, I'm not trespassing. It seems he's hiding out inside."

"It didn't look like he's hiding. He doesn't know we are looking for him. So he doesn't have to panic. Here's a thought though, if he's here where is his car?"

"There are tracks leading around the side so he's more than likely parked it out of view behind the barns."

"He could have heard us drive up on the gravel, but we're not too late. I think he's going to run again. Up to now, we've always been a step too late. Here, come and have a look at this."

Al followed Toby to the garage and Toby showed him the old car.

"Very nice, that's a classic Opel Monza, and it's spotless. Just look at the shine on the bodywork. It's a 'T' registration, I think that's the late 70s, around '78. He certainly looked after it. I'd guessed he collected stuff, but that's a surprise."

"That's what I thought. It's cold, so it's not been used recently. Shall we take it for a spin?"

"You're joking. We don't want to damage it breaking in. It's a criminal offence to steal a car, anyway."

"This place is nice but it must have cost a fortune. I can't see Karl owning it. It's either one of his mates or a family member."

As they came out they heard someone call out from the steps by the main door.

"Hello is someone there?"

Al and Toby stepped out of the garage door and saw a man in a raincoat and wellington boots walking towards them. He looked like he was in his late fifties. A woman stood in the porch by the main door.

"What do you think you are doing? Get out of our garage."

Al went to pacify him. "We're ever so sorry, I knocked but when there was no answer I thought the place was unoccupied."

The man took one look at Al's face under his hood and thought the worst. "That's no excuse you are trespassing on private property. Get away or I'll call the police."

"Is this your hotel?"

"No, I'm the caretaker and that is my wife." Pointing to the woman standing by the door. "We are closed for the season for refurbishment."

"Have you had any visitors recently?"

"That's none of your business. We're closed."

"I am sorry, the garage wasn't locked, I assure you we haven't damaged anything, we are just looking for someone and we heard he might be here."

"I said we are closed so how can we have had any visitors."

"Has the owner been here recently?"

"No, he hasn't been here since last October. I asked you to go."

"Maybe we should ask him. Who is the owner?"

"Are you accusing me of lying?"

Toby suddenly broke in with a pleading voice. "No sir, you said he isn't here but if we could speak to the owner it could help us."

The caretaker visibly softened and looked to his wife, who nodded. "Well okay, it's Mr Prateung."

If it had been daylight Toby would have seen Al's, face go white. Something had just occurred to him.

Toby continued. "It's really important, do you have a contact number we so could call him?"

The caretaker called to his wife to get a card from the reception desk. She brought one, and he gave it to Toby, who showed it to Al. The number was on it and Al tried to memorise it. Then, in case he forgot it, he wrote it down in the notes section on his phone.

Toby was calm. "Thank you, sir, and ma'am, we won't bother you any longer. Come on, we'd better go."

For the benefit of the caretakers, Al said: "Okay let's go, there's nothing here for us." Then quietly to Toby, "I've taken a few photos with my phone."

They climbed into their car, Al drove around the half circular drive turned and waved to the caretakers and drove away. As they turned into the road Al glanced across at Toby. "Thanks Toby, I was getting worried she might be calling the police while he kept us talking."

"No, I watched her, she never took her eyes off us. I think she was ready to though if we caused any trouble. I saw him look at you and panic. You'll have to re-cover those bruises tomorrow. Shall we park round the bend and wait for Karl? He looked ready to go."

"No, I'm tired out after today. It's after midnight and the temperature outside is zero. I'm relying on Ashley to track his next move. We'll catch up with him tomorrow."

"He could be going to the airport."

"Not this time of night. He's going out to a club for the night."

Thirteen

The caretaker turned and strode back to his wife at the door. "Phew that was scary, I'm glad they're gone. What was all that about?"

"Are you okay Mark, you're shaking? You're so brave confronting them. They could have been here to burgle the place. One of them was huge, and the other looked like he's been in a fight."

"I have to tell Karl and I think we should call Mr Prateung and let him know about them. They were searching for something."

"I heard him say, someone, not something."

"Well, whichever I'm calling just to be sure they don't accuse us of anything."

"Come inside dear you need to calm down I'll pour you a drink."

They went inside and Mark was straight on the phone to the owner and explained what had just occurred.

Karl came into the small bar area and confronted them. "What's going on I heard voices outside?"

"Nothing to worry about just a couple of intruders looking around Mark has got rid of them. We've just called Mr Prateung and let him know. I'm sure there's not a problem. We don't expect them to be back."

Karl was suspicious but knew the caretakers wouldn't tell him any more.

Al drove straight back to the Leven River hotel. They found the lounge bar again. It was late and there was only one couple sitting together close to the fire hearth with drinks. So Al chose the easy chairs with a small table. They fancied a nightcap so when the waiter came to them they each ordered whisky with cola.

"Thanks for calming him down Toby, I was getting angry. I'm glad you were there."

"That was close. They could have arrested us for trespass and breaking and entering."

"If he's out for the night, then he'll probably sleep late. We'll be up and ready to go early and hopefully, he buys fuel or something that Ashley can trace."

A light came on in Al's mind, suddenly he knew what had been going on. Now they had problems because if the caretaker had phoned the owner of Lakeview, Decha knew too. He told us he didn't know where Karl was. That he was still searching for him, but Karl is here and Decha owns the place.

*****

Hannah and Eleanor arrived at the nightclub and found an empty table. It was still early for this club, but they knew it would soon be packed with youngsters, trying to find a partner for the night. Especially on a Saturday night. They knew they would probably be the oldest women here, but it was still better than being home alone. They ordered drinks from a waitress who was prowling around with trays. Eleanor wasn't especially interested in spending the night with anyone, but a few drinks and a dance wouldn't hurt.

Karl arrived at the Sidings nightclub, checked his overcoat, and went straight to the bar. He ordered a vodka and tonic, ice no slice, turned and looked around for anyone looking lonely. He felt smart and confident in his new jacket and open-necked silk shirt. The place was pretty quiet but there were a few groups of people sitting at tables around the dance floor.

He saw two women sitting at a table towards the back of the

dance floor. He thought he recognised one from his last visit. He carried his drink and casually approached them.

"Hi, It's Eleanor, isn't it? Remember me, it's Tarik? From last summer."

She remembered him but was so shocked and shaken she didn't respond at first. Pretending not to hear him over the sound of the music. He repeated it louder this time.

"Pardon? Oh yes." She wanted to go. "It's been a while."

The music was loud, so he had to shout. "Who's your friend?"

Eleanor shouted back. "This is Hannah; she's only staying for one drink."

"Hi, Hannah, why don't you stay for a couple?"

"No thanks I've got children at home. Can't leave them too long."

"That's a shame we could have had some fun."

Eleanor was having none of it. "Not tonight Tarik we've just stopped in on our way home." Somehow she had to get a message to Al and Toby. "Would you excuse us a minute we need the ladies' room? Come on, Hannah."

Eleanor led the way and once inside she turned to Hannah. "Oh my god, that's him. He's using a different name though. I think it's the same as last year, although I had forgotten."

"You went white. I thought you'd seen a ghost. Are you sure?" Hannah was thinking about what to do next. "If you're right, we'd better let Al know."

"I am right. You call Al. I'll go back, finish my drink, then make an excuse and leave."

"Will you be all right on your own with him?"

"I'll be fine. He's not dangerous. I'm feeling sick though, probably just shock of seeing him, I'm capable of making excuses."

"Okay if you're sure. I'll call Al and let you know what he says. Please be careful."

"Go. Call me when your home safe."

"Okay let me know when you're home too."

Hannah left for the door without passing Karl on the way out. She stood in the entrance hall and called Al.

****

Al was in the bar with Toby when the call came. He answered straight away.

"Hi, Hannah what's up? Did you both get home okay?"

"Hi, Al we didn't go straight home. Listen, I know it's late but we're in Sidings nightclub. You remember, the one in Ulverston. You won't believe this but Karl just approached us. He remembered Eleanor from last year and asked to join us. He's calling himself Tarik now, although Eleanor says he used that name before but she'd forgotten. She says it's definitely him though."

"You're joking, I thought you would be home and safe by now. Is she okay?"

"She just wanted to let off steam. It shocked her when he came up though, but she's all right now. We went to the ladies, and she told me. I've left her to come and call you."

"Is she on her own with him in there?"

"Yes, but she's okay. She's only having one drink then she'll make excuses to get home early."

"Okay well, I don't think he's dangerous. Just looking for female company tonight."

"I'm waiting for her by the door. If she doesn't come out in five minutes I'm going back in to find her. Then we're off home. We will call each other when we get home so we won't worry all night."

"Good idea. Can you call me too or I will worry?"

****

Eleanor went back to Karl and sat across from him. Sipping her drink, she didn't know what to say, so she asked. "Where have you been hiding? I haven't seen you in here for months."

"Oh here and there. Where's Hannah?"

"She had to go. I told you we were only here for a quick drink."

"But she's left hers. She must be in a hurry to get home."

110

"I'm going when I finish mine too. I feel sick. We had a meal in the Shepherds Inn and I think it has disagreed with me."

"That's a shame I was hoping for your company tonight."

"Well, you're out of luck I wouldn't be much company at the moment, anyway."

He looked annoyed then he stood up. "Fine, I'll see you around then." He left her and went to search elsewhere for some female company.

Eleanor felt so relieved she quickly finished her drink and left. She met Hannah in the foyer. "I thought you had gone home, still waiting for the taxi?"

"No, I called Al then waited for you. I was all ready to come back in to find you when I saw you coming out."

They phoned for a taxi to take them home.

The driver dropped Hannah first then carried on to Eleanor's house. When she got there, she called Hannah to say she was safe and to tell Al Karl was still in the club when she left.

****

Karl was up early after a blowout night at the club. He couldn't find anyone looking for company. No one-night stands or lonely people like him, after late night fun. He didn't wait for breakfast deciding to stop on the way. Overnight rain had cleared, and It was milder. He drove away from the lake district back down the M6 motorway. Past places he only knew as rugby teams. Wigan, St Helens, Warrington. Onto the M56 motorway past Widnes and Ellesmere Port into Wales.

It was his first time in Wales and he didn't know what to expect. He assumed it was much like England and it was. More strange names though. Tomorrow was the day of the auction so he'd planned to check it out before the day. He stopped for breakfast at a place called Mold and checked the auction rooms brochure again while he ate. He had already registered his bank account with the auctioneers so he could bid without any problems. He knew the auctioneers were famous but couldn't believe they had a facility in the town of Bwlch-y-cibau. Checking the route on his phone he calculated it was about an hour further on. He would need to bypass Wrexham but he wasn't in a hurry.

****

Al called Toby from the room phone to suggest they didn't go for breakfast as Karl may see them. He wanted to check out, and if necessary, check back into the Shepherds Inn. He suggested they meet in reception where he made a quick call to Ashley. "Hi, Ash any ideas where Karl is?"

"Yes, he's in Wales."

"*Wales*, how did he get there so fast? My god, he's leading us a merry dance."

"He must have stopped at a small rest area in a place called Mold because he bought food."

"Don't go anywhere. I'll talk to Toby and call you back."

"Sure." They hung up and Al told Toby.

"Toby, Karl is in Wales. He stopped for breakfast in a place called Mold early this morning."

"*What.* He must have left at the crack of dawn to get there by now. Let's be honest we don't know where he's going." Toby was furious. "I knew we should have stopped him going out last night. We'll never catch him now."

"It will be okay." He was thinking aloud. "There's no point going back to the Shepherds Inn then." He needed a quick way to Wales. "I'm not done yet I may know a way to get in front of him."

"How? We'll need a helicopter."

"Maybe you're right."

He made another call to see if he could get one. To stop Toby moaning too much.

"Hannah is Brian still around?"

"The pilot?"

"Yes, we need to borrow him and his plane for a short flight."

"He's still here. I'll give him a ring and see if he's busy."

"Tell him to drop everything. I'll make it worth his while. Oh, and tell him it's one only way too."

"I'll call and ask him, tell him where you're going."

"Anglesey. Call me back ASAP it's urgent."

Fourteen

It was twenty miles to Walney Airfield, and they drove as fast as they dared in the treacherous, snow-covered roads without losing the car on black ice. They did it in forty minutes. They saw the large nondescript hanger reflected in the bright snowy fields. They parked in the deserted the airfield, close to the hanger and waited in the car because they were exposed to a hellish, Irish sea wind, blowing in from the sea. Before the pilot arrived Al got a call into Neil to ask him to arrange a hire car at Anglesey Airport. He'd forgotten about transport when they got there.

Neil took ages answering and when he eventually did, he apologised, blaming the phone.

"I'm not very good with technology you know that, what can I do for you?

He surprised Neil at the request. "Anglesey, what are you up to now?"

"It's a long story. Text me the details when you know them. There's no point calling me back the plane is too noisy."

"A noisy plane, what's going on, are you crazy?"

"I'm not flying it we're just passengers. Message me okay?"

"Right, I'll sort that for you, how are you getting on?"

"We're ok. I can't talk now, get that sorted ASAP and I'll call later. We'll be there in about an hour so it's urgent."

They didn't have to wait long before the pilot arrived, rolled out of his car, collected his walking stick and limped towards the hangar. He opened the hangar doors so they could get in out if the wind. Waiting inside was a small four-seater aircraft.

Toby and Al picked up their bags, put up their hoods and trudged to the hangar doors.

Al shook the pilot's hand as he arrived at the door. "Thanks, Brian, this is a great help."

"You're lucky it's a Sunday. I enjoy taking her up at the weekends. It's a good thing you've only got backpacks too. She only has a small luggage compartment."

Toby pulled Al to one side and said as quietly as he could, "Are you sure about this Al, it looks like something from the last war."

Brian was proud of his prize possession "I heard that. It's a Grumman Tiger AA-5B, made in '74."

"Seventy-four years ago. It's like a Spitfire," Toby said.

"It is not, she's a four-seater made for touring, only 40 years old."

"She's older than me."

Brian limped towards his plane then turned and said.

"Do you want to go or not? Come on, help me get in onto the runway."

"How? You mean you want us to push it?"

"I'm not allowed to start her in the hangar and she's too heavy for me on my own with this leg."

"Of course, we'll help, won't we Toby?" Al said digging him in the ribs. "We need his help."

They pushed the small plane out of the hangar onto the runway. The plane weighed fifteen hundred pounds, had a wingspan of thirty-one and a half feet, was eight feet tall and twenty-two feet long. Toby still thought it was a relic from the last war.

Brian used portable steps, climbed in and started the engine. Al and Toby clambered aboard over the wing. Al sat next to Brian and Toby sat behind him. With only four seats it was tight inside, so Toby, needing the legroom, sat sideways. He needed one and a half seats.

No luxury this time thought Al. He hoped Toby would be okay after the last flight. The seats weren't comfortable and there wasn't a refreshment trolley. He felt a thrill though as the propeller turned.

Above the roar of the aeroplane's engine, Brian shouted. "Buckle up, it might be jerky at first."

They finally got going at ten thirty. The little craft turned gently, advancing along the runway, constantly picking up speed until it reached eight-hundred and fifty feet per minute and effortlessly rose upward in a steep take-off and soared into the pale blue sky. While still climbing, Brian turned and banked the plane to the left in a southerly direction. As the aircraft ascended over Northwest England Toby watched the wintry fields slink away and the smooth silvery water appear. They hit an air pocket and were buffeted about.

Toby was taking pictures with his phone as they took off. He had to shout to be heard, he leaned across the front seats. "I've never been in a small plane before, it's strange to be so close to the pilot."

"We'll be flying below the clouds, so you can see the land all the way," Brian said.

"Wow, all the way?"

"Well, you could except we will be over the sea for most of the way, but you will see the coast."

All Al could see in front of him was a clear blue cloudless sky.

Brian was running through operations and manoeuvres, turning left and right checking instruments. "You're quiet Alain."

"It's a wonderful view, but I'm thinking about what to do when we arrive."

He had a load on his mind and didn't want to reveal how tense he was.

Toby was fascinated with the little plane. "What is the range of this thing?" Toby asked.

"Around seven hundred and fifty miles If we keep the speed to two fifty kilometres an hour."

"It doesn't seem that fast when you're up here. What's with the leg?"

"I broke it in a car accident twenty years ago, ask Al I'm sure he remembers."

"Right, I'll ask him when we have a quiet moment."

Toby had no idea how high they were, but he guessed at two thousand feet. They were passing over the Irish Sea, to their right in the distance beyond the oil and gas platforms lay the Isle of Man, and to their left the English coast and the seaside town of Blackpool

"From this far up the coast looks beautiful," Al said, "I had to do a survey of the area for an advertising company a few years back. We picked up a chopper from Lytham St Anne's heliport at Blackpool airport out to the Morecambe Bay gas platforms."

"I remember that. I flew you down to Blackpool a few times." Said Brian.

"Yes, you came home all puffed up because you'd been in a helicopter," Toby said.

"Oh shut up, you'd have been the same."

"Yeh, yeh, yeh, I know, but it was funny how you boasted about it."

"It was funny looking back, not at the time though. I was late arriving at the heliport so I got the last jumpsuit. I think it was meant for you Toby, it was extra-large, and it drowned me. I had to roll the legs up and stuff them in my boots, then fold the arms back. I looked lost in that bright orange getup."

"Good to be seen though, in case of emergencies," Brian said.

Al shut up then and looked at the scenery from the window on his left. As they continued south, he could see the distant port of Liverpool with two huge cruise ships, which sat motionless in the grey water. He was thinking how beautifully green England was when he realised he was probably looking down upon Wales.

Eventually, Brian took the plane down in a gradual descent and landed perfectly on the runway at Anglesey Airport. Where a ground staff person welcomed them.

Once they were all on the ground Al paid Brian and thanked him. "Thanks again for this Brain. I've asked Hannah to take our car home. Here are the keys. I'll be back for it as soon as I can. We'll go for a drink when I get back."

"No problem, anytime you're free I'm up for a pint or two."

There are no hire car offices at Anglesey airport, so Neil had arranged a meet and greet service from Hertz. They got an Astra five-door hatch, almost brand new. Well, the mileage was so low it looked like they had wound the clock back. Almost impossible to have driven anywhere since leaving the factory.

Toby took the wheel so Al plugged his phone into the cigar lighter to charge it during the drive. Then he made a quick call to Ashley. "Hi, Ash any ideas where Karl is now?"

"He continued on to a place called Bwlch-y-cibau. It's in Llanfyllin, where he's booked into a small hotel called the Valley Guest House."

"Where? There are some weird town names in Wales. That sounds ominous I wonder why he's gone there?"

"No Idea. I'm searching for the area on the internet right now. If I find anything relevant, I'll call you."

"Thanks. Keep it up we're not far behind him now."

He checked his maps app to establish the distance and time it would take to get to Llanfyllin.

He turned to Toby. "Ashley says he's at a hotel in one of your weirdly named places called Bwlch-y-cibau. I've found it. I reckon we'll make there in a couple of hours."

"Let's get moving then, shall we? Can we stop for a bite to eat on the way, I'm starving?"

They drove in silence and Toby allowed Al to close his eyes and rest. During the drive, he was trying to remember something he'd heard recently about Karl. It wouldn't come to him. It seemed to him he was always out of their reach. Every time they got close, he moved. Like a moving target, he wouldn't stay still long enough for them to catch him. He was deep in thought until he stopped in Pentrefoelas for a comfort break. He woke Al and they found an inn with a bar overlooking a lake, to buy breakfast.

"I've never been to Wales, have you?" Toby asked when they were seated.

"Once, when I was about twenty. I can't remember much about it."

"On holiday?"

"Yes, with a load of mates. My girlfriend at the time, her mate had an uncle who owned a big house. So about ten of us stayed for a week."

"I remember now. I was about eleven. I envied you going away without mum and dad. I couldn't wait to go without them. I didn't know it was here though. My first trip was to Eastbourne."

After a breakfast bap and coffee, they moved on. That niggling feeling was back and Toby he was tiring having driven for almost two hours when they stopped in the small town of Llanfyllin. It was about three miles from the last known location for Karl. They tried to check into the Llanfyllin Valley Hotel but were too early, so the receptionist asked them to come back at three o'clock when check-in opened. They registered anyway and promised to be back. Then returned their bags to the boot of the car and went to check out Bwlch-y-cibau. There was only one road into the town and on the way, they passed the Pull Inn. It looked like a typical country pub with real ale and food cooked all day. It was as good a place as any to ask around for local knowledge. Maybe Karl was just stopping off for the night as part of a long journey, or there was another reason for being here. They continued on through the village to look around.

Toby wasn't sure what was going on here. "Blink and you'll miss it."

"It's a strange place to stop isn't it."

Toby turned the car around and headed back to the Pull Inn.

It was two thirty when they entered the pub and Al went straight to the bar while Toby went to the toilets. He ordered pints of local beer each, and a Sunday roast from the carvery each. Then carried the beer to a table set for four and waited for Toby. The place had a cosy feel, there were half of the dozen tables in use with a few locals enjoying their food. When Toby arrived, he demolished his beer in two mouthfuls, then went to buy another. The alcohol dulled the agony in his back and arms and made him light-headed. As far as he was concerned, Al could drive from now on.

The journey had tired them so they both wanted to take it easy for a few hours, ask around. Then go back and check in to their hotel and call Ash.

The landlord had covered the pub walls with copies of paintings from famous artists. At least they looked like copies. Al thought it was risky to hang real ones here in this small village. There were scented candles and a roaring fire too. A nice little public house in a quaint place. Toby was right again you would miss it if you were travelling too fast through it.

Toby thought it would be a good idea to find out what was going on around. It might help explain why Karl was here. "I'll have a chat with the landlord, country neighbours are closer than you think. They rely on each other, know each other's business. They could help us out."

"Good idea, I'll sit here, drink this pint and think, while I wait."

"What's up with you?"

"I didn't sleep well last night; my bruises are telling me to rest. I didn't expect any of this. I didn't think it would be so hard to sort this out. I Just want to catch up with him and get this over with."

"You've got your ticket for the carvery if you want to queue up. I won't be long." He went to the bar.

Al used his phone to surf the internet for a while then drank another mouthful of his beer and joined the food line.

Toby took his beer to the bar, found a barstool and asked the barman what, if anything, was happening around the place in the next few days.

The bartender was filling shelves with clean glasses from a plastic box. He stopped and came over to answer Toby's question. "Not much going on in this place. Most folks are farmers and they keep to themselves. Are you here for the auction?"

"Auction, no, what auction? I'm here scouting the area for locations with my brother over there." He pointed to Al in the food queue. "We work for a motion picture production company."

"I saw you come in. Your brother has been in a flight, has he?"

"He was mugged last week, by a group of thugs. He's still recovering from the beating. I'm sure he'll be okay; he needs to rest."

"It's a lovely village to hide in if that's what you're after, it's small and tucked away. We only have a corner shop, this pub and an auction house. Not much action. We don't have hotels so most people stay outside in Llanfyllin or Llanfechain. There are a couple of bed and breakfast places, just for visitors to the auctions.

"We have one a week and they are hotly contested. We love it, it brings folks to the pub. The auction keeps us going really, be just locals without it. It's called Sothebys so people get confused, they think it's part of the big famous one in London, ours has an S on the end, the London place doesn't, they add an apostrophe.

"People come for miles around. Many to buy and some to watch. There's a lot of visitors this weekend because it's stamp day tomorrow. They are very expensive; I've seen them go for thousands. There's a pamphlet on the small table by the door if you're interested."

"Yes, we looked for a hotel but ended up staying in Llanfyllin. Thanks for the insight, we might go and watch. The food looks great. I'll have another pint of this while you're not busy."

He picked up a pamphlet and his fresh pint, took them to the table, then joined the carvery queue. He couldn't get much more on his plate when so joined Al at their table, who was well into his dinner and his pint.

"Find out anything? Any ideas why Karl is here?"

"Not much around here but there is an auction tomorrow and apparently it's stamp day."

"Really? We ought to go and find out if he's here to buy anything."

"Here's a list of what's on offer. He's going to need a lot of money if he intends to buy something from this little lot."

"I looked up that watch Eleanor was on about by the way. I think it's a Jaeger Lecoultre and they range from three and a half thousand up to thirty thousand."

"It sounds like he can afford what's on offer tomorrow then."

At a quarter to two the following day Karl sat in the middle row of the auction room waiting patiently for them to call Lot 117. When he'd arrived he thought, this place is weird. He was expecting a flash house or office considering the reserves of the lots. Instead, the whole place needs a facelift, it was old and tatty. Still, what do you expect in a small town in Wales, he thought? He must be in the right place.

The room was full of buyers. They looked to him like they came from all backgrounds, some were smartly dressed, after the expensive stuff, he reckoned. A few in anoraks, a load in tweedy coats, looked like farmers, come to watch maybe. Still, at least it's full, all the seats are taken so there were people standing at the side walls or at the back. All types of bidders, some talking on their mobile phones, quite a lot with numbered paddles like him.

Most of the lots were, in his opinion, bric-à-brac, not worth travelling to the auction. What surprised him was the things people bid for. It all seemed worthless to him. Then again, he had never been into antiques so he hadn't a clue of the value. Except for Lot 117 which he hoped was worth his freedom.

Not that he was a prisoner or anything it was just that he felt his life was being planned for him and he felt someone watching him. Like those guys who helped Tesanee when the police turned up. He knew they were following him. Still, just this auction then he could get the stamp and get it to his uncle. Then he would be free to go anywhere, do anything. He could become anybody he wanted to be. He'd done it before and he'd do it again.

He took the catalogue from his suit pocket and read it again. It looked legitimate. 'Auctioneers and Valuers of Collectables since 1958' it said. 'Coins, Banknotes, Medals & Militaria, Postcard, Stamps & Postal History', all sorts of expensive antique stuff. The lots in their stamp auctions were subject to the 1985 revision of the Philatelic Auctioneers Standard Terms and Conditions. He'd looked this up and was satisfied it was authentic.

The stamp he was after was a valuable Chinese stamp issued in 1968, during Chairman Mao's revolution. It featured a man holding Mao's Little Red Book. It was famous because it has a flaw with the printing. It should be all red but has some white to the right of the picture.

He scanned the room and tried to judge the buyers, they all seemed jittery. They all looked so different he couldn't tell who was willing to pay high prices or had the means to afford the most expensive items, who would keep raising the cost with no regard to money. He knew he could get it though, no matter who bid against him or how much.

At least it was a closed room with no commission bids and no internet bidding. He couldn't stop the phone bids though, he just had to go with the flow. He thought they had set a high reserve price, so he knew it was going to cost him a lot, but It was make or break for him.

Fifteen

All the seats were taken, so Al and Toby stood at the back of the auction room by the main doors, scanning the room too. Both had tried to change their appearance. They looked like a couple of hikers. Al was dressed in a dark blue North Face jacket with blue jeans. Toby was in a black, unbranded, quilted jacket with a hood and black denim jeans. They both wore hiking boots. Al had removed Hannah's makeup, he'd taken the paper stitches off and had grown two days' stubble, his black eye had faded some. Toby had his hood up.

They saw Karl sitting in the middle row. He was fidgeting with his phone and reading the catalogue.

Al whispered to Toby. "He's on his own in there, looking around nervously, and by the look of him he's never been to an auction before."

"Looks about right. He can't keep still he's looking around trying to assess the other bidders. He's definitely new to this. Like me. I haven't got a clue how these things work."

"We don't have to do anything let's let him bid and see how far he can go. See how much he's prepared to spend."

"Have you seen the catalogue? Any idea what he's likely to bid for?"

"I have a theory but nothing definite."

Unbeknown to Al and Toby, Karl had seen them at the back of the auction room. He couldn't worry about them at the moment though, this was far too important. They would have to wait until after the auction.

He had a plan to escape them anyway, so he concentrated on the auctioneer and listening for Lot 117. When the auctioneer called Lot 100, he asked the man sitting on his left if he would look after his set for him while he excused himself and went to the toilet. After using the facilities, he went to the back storage room and asked if there was another way out of the building. He used the excuse that if he managed a successful bid he wanted to leave without being seen. The backroom staff understood and showed him the way to the back exit door. When he returned to his seat, he had missed five lots.

It seemed like an age getting to Lot 117. In fact, he'd been waiting an hour and a half. It was three twenty-five when the auctioneer called the number. At last, he thought, the time has arrived. They presented the stamp behind a glass screen and magnified it for easy viewing then put it on an easel. His excitement was building, he was alert and adrenalin pumped through him. The auctioneer started the bidding at fifty thousand pounds. Oh well, here we go he thought, no turning back now, and he raised his arm.

The bidding went up quickly at first in increments of ten thousand pound steps. Until it reached one hundred thousand. Then it slowed and soon there were only four bidders remaining. A young girl in her twenties from the left side on the phone. A really smart looking woman from the front row, who he liked the look of, and a short smug looking man, with fair hair and a clipped moustache, two rows in front of him. The room was totally silent; it fascinated everyone to see the way the bidding was flowing back and forward, side to side.

He had a limit, but he wasn't anywhere near it yet. The auctioneer upped the bidding to fifty thousand each step. This sent a gasp around the room. Still, he kept pace with the others. The woman at the front gave up at two hundred and fifty thousand. The three surviving bidders raised the price to five hundred thousand. The smug looking man two rows up turned and looked at Karl, then shook his head, bowing out at six-hundred thousand. When the bid approached a million the auctioneer had to silence the room with a slam of his gavel. The room quietened down and he began again. The last bidder, the young girl on the phone, matched him up to one million four hundred and fifty thousand pounds and then paused, asking her contact on the phone whether she should continue. She shook her head to show she had finished. The Auctioneer banged his gavel three times and Karl and his stamp.

Someone clapped and the whole room burst into applause. He was so emotional he could have cried with happiness. It would shock his uncle when he presented him with the rarest Chinese stamp ever printed. The whole country was indeed red.

Toby followed the proceedings in utter amazement. It was so exciting he thought his jaw was probably drooping. He was absolutely astounded at the way the bidding went. It never occurred to him Karl had so much money or he would spend so much on a stamp. They had pursued him all this way, and he wanted to buy a stamp.

How much is he worth, he thought. If he can afford to invest that kind of money in an afternoon on a stamp, he ought to be able to repay Tesanee too. When the auction is over, I am going to make him pay her back.

Al beckoned to him to leave, and they left the room and headed to the car park.

"I can't believe what I've just watched in there."

"I know Toby; I'm just as astonished as you."

"We've got to catch him, Al. He needs to pay her back and I know he can with all the money he must have. I had no clue he was so rich."

"Come on, let's get to the car before he comes out. We've got him in sight now. We'll let him leave then follow him."

****

Karl left by the back door, determined to get away. Desperate to get back to Lakeview and contact his uncle. He had just paid out a fortune and he needed to trade his newest possession for his freedom. All he had to do was convince his uncle it was worth it, then he was sure he would agree and allow his freedom. He needed to walk away without ever looking over his shoulder again.

He looked around the car park and couldn't see those two guys or anyone else there to stop him. In his excitement, he accelerated too quickly as he turned out causing himself to brake hard at the first corner. It was slippery, so the tyres slid on some black ice and he almost lost it. He slowed the car down and managed to keep it on the road. As soon as he turned the corner the tyres gripped, and he sped away.

As soon as Karl had left his seat to pay, Al and Toby went out to their car. They had parked it at the rear of the car park away from the doors. Karl had parked his car at the front, near the exit.

They expected him to come from the front doors so they sat and watched. Suddenly Toby spotted him making his way from the back of the building. When he reached his car, they watched him open the boot and put a parcel in. They waited for him to drive out of the car park.

Al started their car and pulled out after him. He could see the rear brake lights of the BMW as it turned the first corner and saw it skid. Karl was driving at such a pace it was difficult to keep up. He could certainly handle the country roads well. On these country lanes, it would be difficult to see the black car so he was pleased it was still daylight for another hour at least. There were no other cars on the road as he drove out of the village and into the lanes.

He knew Toby had wanted to confront him as they left the auction room but he'd not wanted to draw attention to them with so many people around. He preferred to stop him on a quiet road or at a refreshment area. He followed at a safe distance so that Karl wouldn't suspect being followed.

Karl drove at a steady pace keeping to the speed limits, convinced he was safe. Al kept up with him along the windy lanes until they reached the busy main road. A left turn and a faster road.

After fifteen minutes they were well on their way north. They passed into England for a couple of miles before passing back into Wales.

Toby was getting anxious. "It looks like he's heading back to Lakeview." He couldn't wait to stop him and make him pay for all the hurt he'd done to Al and Tesanee.

"He's certainly in a hurry. It's a good job we checked out of the hotel earlier. We would have no chance of keeping up with him if we hadn't."

Karl turned onto a stretch of road that had earlier been covered with ice and almost lost the rear of the car in a spin. He fought to keep it in a straight line. Al came round the bend and saw him slipping and sliding so he braked hard and oversteered to counter for the slippery road. He almost crashed into the rear of Karl's car.

Karl saw them in the rear-view mirror and tried to speed up to no avail, the wheels spun with little or no traction or forward movement. Al kept the car from spinning but stalled it. In his haste to restart it, Karl straightened up and drove on, turned another corner and they lost sight of him.

It took a few goes, but he managed to start it and drove on. At the next bend, they saw the taillights of the BMW again. The roads were treacherous, and no matter how hard he tried Al could not catch it. He decided to be sensible and let Karl go.

"I can't catch him, Toby."

"Do you want to change over? I'll drive if you want."

"No, it looks like he's heading back to Lakeview. The roads are too slippery; I don't want to kill us trying to catch him. We'll find him again I'm sure."

Just then they heard a crashing sound in the distance, it sounded like a car hitting a wall. Toby urged Al to keep going to see if it was Karl. Maybe they would get lucky and he wasn't too far ahead.

They turned two more corners and caught up with Karl. He had skidded into a bridge support post and was trying to manoeuvre his car away from a corner post. AL drove up behind him to stop him reversing. Toby was out of the car in a flash and ran towards Karl. Before he could get around the cars to him Karl's door flew open and Karl jumped out and ran back towards Al.

Al stepped out of the car onto the road to see Karl running straight into him screaming. "What do you want from me? I don't understand why are you chasing me?"

Al didn't have time to answer him as Karl ducked and grabbed Al around the midriff. His strong arms encircling Al's waist while his shoulder was on Al's hip pushing him backwards.

They both hit the ground. Al was hitting Karl on the back but with a shove, Al was on the grass verge. One more push and he was sliding down the bank beside the road, on his back. He struggled to turn over and get up on his knees, but he could feel momentum pulling at him, he felt himself pick up speed heading downhill. He managed to turn and get up then lost his balance and fell forward, his face thudding into the ground.

Toby got round to Karl as Al was tumbling downwards. He pulled Karl backwards, pushed past him and shoved him back into the road. He went after Al to catch him before he reached the bottom of the bank.

Karl got up, looked at them for a few seconds then said: "Get away from me."

Then he raced back to his car, jumped in, reversed back into Al and Toby's car to make space, before speeding away across the bridge. He was thinking, I need to escape, to get back to my 'haven' in Cumbria.

Toby slid down the bank and reached out to Al helping him up.

"Are you all right?"

Al had scratches on his face and hands but his coat had taken the brunt of the fall.

"Yes, it was so sudden, he was on me before I could do

anything. I overbalanced and lost my footing. Then the hill took me. I couldn't slow down."

"He's gone. Let me get you to the hospital. You look terrible again. Just when I thought you had recovered from the last beating this happens. I will never live this down."

"You're okay, only your pride is hurt, it's me who's been in the wars."

Sixteen

Karl was exhausted when he arrived at Lakeview after the long, four-hour drive. It was late evening by the time he parked and went to the door, only to receive a frosty reception. Mark opened it and stood aside to let him in.

As he passed Mark welcomed him with. "Welcome back Mr Hurnston, have you eaten? We could prepare something quick for you."

"I'm fine, thank you. I need a drink though."

Mark sensed Karl's mood but didn't press it. "There's someone waiting in the lounge for you."

Alison stood directly behind Mark and Karl saw the expression on her face. She looked afraid as if he freighted her. There was something in Mark's tone that unsettled him too.

"Oh! who is it?"

"See for yourself."

"I will thanks. What's up with you two, anyway?"

He strode into the lounge and was startled to discover who it was. Two men both holding whisky glasses and cigars. One he recognised, staring straight him, and one he couldn't fully make out, sitting in an armchair with his back turned towards him. They looked like they had been here a while, there was a roaring fire in the fireplace.

"Uncle Decha! how are you.?"

"I'm quite well thank you. I've brought someone with me. He's here to see you too."

He stared across to the corner chair and the other man turned towards him. His heart skipped a beat. This didn't feel good. "Papa! what are you doing here?"

"Hello, Karit."

"Call me Karl. I've been Karl for a long time, and I prefer it, and can we speak English."

"Okay, English then. You are my son and I named you Karit. It is your name, and that's what I will call you."

"What do you want?"

"I've learned many things about you, and I wished to find out for myself. From you."

"What things. What have you been telling him, uncle?"

"The truth Karit, the truth."

The anger showed on his face, these men had bullied him all his life. Well, not anymore. "Truth, what truth are you talking about?"

"Your father is concerned for your wellbeing. He's travelled a long way to help you."

"I don't need helping. I'm managing all on my own, thank you."

Karit's father raised his voice saying. "Sit down and explain why you have been stealing from your uncle and your partner."

"I don't have to explain anything to anybody. Especially for you. I am going up to my room to take a shower. I've been travelling all day, and I am tired. When I'm ready, we will talk. I'm not a child anymore."

He stormed out and went to his room.

Karit's father went to refill his glass. Then he turned to apologise to Decha in their native language, Cebuano.

"I'm sorry about my son, he's always been impetuous. He gets it from me, I think. You know him by now."

"Yes, I notice how he becomes fired up about the smallest insignificant detail."

"Seeing us must be a shock he's tired and angry. It shows he is human; he has made decisions he can't change. Like most people, he will defend them or shut them out and not speak of them. It's a family trait."

"Yes you did shock him, he's lost my swagger. Let him calm down." He smiled.

"I will speak with him when he returns. Let us have another drink. It's good to see you after all these years."

"Yes, it is good, I'm sorry it has to be under difficult circumstances."

"It's always good to see old friends, no matter what has arisen."

Karl was furious when he got to his room. He threw his coat on a chair, went straight to the bathroom and turned on the shower. Then and undressed, tossing his clothes on the bed. He stepped into the shower, feeling the jets of warm water peel the journey off him. What was the matter with him, every time he thought he was getting somewhere something else turned up?

After drying himself he sat on the bed and waited a few minutes until he had calmed down. He hadn't expected his father to turn up. Why had his uncle thought to involve him? Just the thought reminded him of his dad's wicked temper. The memory came at him like a ghost in his dreams.

He had decisions to make, should he tell his uncle about the stamp while his father is here or pretend all is okay and wait for him to leave? He had no choice but to admit it all to his father and find out what he intended to do about it.

He could make out to his uncle as if he would carry on reporting back to him. Leave well alone and wait until his father left. Offer to settle things with Tesanee. Then offer to give him the stamp as repayment for the money he had stolen. Ask him to release him from his debt.

Another thing crossed his mind. What if his father knew nothing about his deal with his uncle? He might not know his uncle had blackmailed him into working for him, spying on Tesanee. They seemed to be friends though so he must know. He thought about it and decided to play it by ear and see what the outcome is. Oh well, into the lion's den as they say.

He dressed, put the parcel in his pocket then returned to

the lounge and went straight to the bar to pour himself a drink. Wary of his father, as he sat down in one of the plush chairs.

He has had aged a bit, he thought, but he looks distinguished in his pale blue suit and his short grey hair, stylish glasses. He looks so fit. He hadn't seen him for nearly ten years. Since his Uncle Decha sent him to England.

He looked up at him. "You look well, father. So what do you want?"

Both men eyed him, swirling their drinks, then they looked at each other. Decha nodded to Karl's' father.

"Uncle Decha tells me you have stolen from him. Is this true?"

"Do you not believe him? I thought you two were friends?"

"Of course I believe him; I want you to tell me yourself."

"You want me to admit it, and then what? You will punish me. Is that it?"

"Karit you need to admit your faults. Not to me, to yourself."

"Why, will it make any difference?"

"If you do, it may help you to stop and start doing things for yourself. Rather than taking from others."

"Okay, I'll stop. Is that what you wanted to hear?"

"Good, but you have to believe it Karit. Really believe it. No more false promises," Decha said.

"I can't turn back the clock, but I can repay my debts."

Another look between his two relatives. "Can you? Repay the debts?" his father asked.

"I know, I've been stupid. Like father like son, Yeh. I told Uncle Decha last week. I've realised I can't keep doing it. So I want to show you I can stop. I tried to explain to him before I came to England but he wouldn't listen. He said I had a debt to him and because I couldn't pay it straight away, I had to repay it by coming here and paying it back over a period of time. Well, I think that time is up and I've repaid him by now."

"Do you now? Well, let me tell you it is an honour to serve the family. It is our custom to always respect your parents or any elder member of your family. So if uncle Decha desires to give you a job you should be thankful to him."

He could have been talking to deaf people. They listened to what he said, they just didn't understand.

"You people just don't get it, do you?" That's so old fashioned. People want to break away from 'the traditions'. We are in the twenty-first century now. I want to be a free man. Free to choose my own way. Be my own person. Free from family commitments, I want to make my own family."

Would he ever get through to them? They can't change, it's in their upbringing. It's a respect thing that goes back centuries. He had to try for his own sake.

"Dad, I want you to be proud of me. Proud that I can be a success on my own merit. Without Uncle Decha or any other family member propping me up. I know I can but you've had no faith in me. In fact, you have had nothing to do with me for most of my adult life. Have you?"

"I am not a perfect father or a perfect man, for that matter, but I am still your father and I am proud of you. What father would not be proud of his son. You have grown to be a fine person but you have to stop what you are doing and learn to live with what you earn not by taking that which is not yours."

"Right, like you then."

"That was wrong of me and it was a long time ago. I have learnt my lesson and served my time so you should learn from me too."

"Don't do as I do. Do as I say. Is that it? It seems I have learnt the wrong things then. Doesn't it?"

"Okay, I hold my hands up I've done things wrong and I've had to pay for them. You say you can repay, then let's see how you intend to do it."

Decha had been quiet for a while. Now though, he could see his investment disappearing. He wondered how Karit would get out of his grasp.

Karl told them about the stamp and counted on his father to support him and persuade Uncle Decha it is worth more than he owed. To allow the debt to be forgotten. It was his only way out; it was all he had. He had to trust his father would see it too.

He took the parcel from his pocket and gave it to his uncle.

"Here uncle, take this in return for the debt I owe you."

"What is this? You owe me much more than this small package Karit."

"Take a look inside and then you will understand it is worth more than I owe you, uncle."

Decha showed it to Karl's father.

"What do you make of it? He seems to think it's all a joke."

"Look inside uncle. I assure you it will be a pleasant surprise. My way of saying sorry and as repayment for stealing from you. I am sorry."

"Do as he says, Decha, unwrap it and look inside."

Decha put his glass down on the bar and untied the small box contained within the wrapping. When he saw the box, he gave a small gasp and open the lid.

"What have you done Karit?"

"Do you like it? Is it the one you told me about?"

"This cannot be real. Look Kunchai."

"It can't be that stamp. Everybody has been searching for a copy. Only a few were ever printed. It's extremely precious and incredibly scarce. Karit where did you get it?"

"At an auction father. I bid for it this afternoon that's where I've been for the last two days. I knew Uncle Decha always wanted it. So when I learned it had come up for auction I bought it for him."

"Where was the auction room?"

"In Wales at Sotheby's auction rooms. They have a massive selection of things there. Hundreds of stamps."

"You are a fool Karit," Decha said. "This cannot be real. It would cost more money than you could afford. I cannot see how it could have been in a small auction in Wales. They would single something like this out for the main showroom in London."

"I have the brochure in my room. I will bring it."

He left them to scrutinise the valuable stamp while he raced upstairs to find the brochure in his overcoat pocket.

When he returned, they had poured another drink each.

"Here look at this, it shows lots of stamps. This one is Lot 117."

"I still cannot believe it. It looks real enough but I will have to have it authenticated by a specialist. I know a couple who come to my club."

"Just think what your friends will say when they see it. Together with all the others in your collection. They will envy you and everyone will think highly of you."

"If this is real, how did you pay for it. The last one sold for over a million dollars."

"It doesn't matter how I paid for it. Does it show I've paid you back?"

"I will get it valued and if it is real, then we will see if I accept it as payment."

He couldn't believe it. They always doubted him. He realised they would never see his point of view. He could never escape. He will always be indebted to the family. Never to be free to live his life on his terms. He knew he would have to run away again. This time they would never find him.

"You will never let me go, will you? I have tried to repay you and you still want to keep me under your thumb. You've got the stamp and I know it's worth more than I owe you." He slammed his glass down on the bar and stormed out.

Kunchai looked apologetic again. "There he goes again. I used to be like that when I was young. The English call it pig-headed. He said it, Like father like son."

"We were all young once." Replied Decha.

A few moments later they heard the main door slam and a car start.

Decha called to Mark. Who came into the lounge and said, "He has taken the Monza, sir."

"Get Praves and Atid. I need them now."

When the two bodyguards arrived, he told them to go after Karl. "Karit has taken my Opel Monza. Bring him back I want him here. And I want the car back without a scratch."

They hurried out into the cold night air.

"Where can he go?" asked Kunchai.

Mark answered from the hallway "He hasn't taken his coat, Mr Kunchai. On a night like this, it's dangerous in these freezing temperatures. Morecambe Bay is a treacherous place at night. Locals claim that when the tide comes in, it does so at a speed that would overtake and submerge a galloping horse. Don't worry though, the boys will find him."

Karl had damaged his car in the crash with the bridge post in Wales. The front sidelight on the passenger side had smashed, but the headlight had escaped damage. The bumper was loose and flapping. Therefore, he couldn't drive it, so he had borrowed his uncle's Opel Monza. He didn't think Uncle Decha or his father would jump in a car and chase after him so he wasn't concerned when a car travelling fast came into his rear-view mirror.

By the time Praves and Atid caught up with Karl he was in Greenodd. "That's him. There is only one car like the Monza around here," said Atid.

Praves was impatient, he had been watching his favourite TV program. "Good! I want to get this over with quickly. It's freezing out there tonight."

The road ahead was empty. Karl was trying to get to the M6 motorway, then he could disappear. This damn road is like a cul-de-sac, one way in and one way out. He drove past the Lakeland Motor Museum onto Newby Bridge.

Then they tried to pass him but there were bends in the road ahead. He kept his speed the same thinking the boy racers would have to wait to pass. By the time they reached Lindale they had had enough and tried their luck.

There was a long left-turn in the road and they were on the wrong side. Praves pulled alongside and Atid gestured for him to let them pass. He slowed slightly, and they went ahead. Narrowly missing a car coming towards them, horns blaring. He was following them now.

All of a sudden, they stopped. Forcing him to swerve and stall his car. Praves and Atid got out of their car and came towards him. The realisation struck him, they had been sent after him by his uncle. He frantically tried to re-start his car. It took three goes to start. He drove past them. They ran back and got in their car.

Karl continued on then turned off the main road into an unlit road leading to the coast. Praves drove past the turning but soon realised there were no red rear lights on the road ahead. So he turned around and found the only turning they had passed.

It was pitch dark as Karl drove on. Past Grange-Over-Sands on to Kents Bank. He caught sight of their headlights just as he arrived in the village.

During low tide, hikers could walk the eight miles across the bay from Kents Bank to Arnside. Karl knew nothing about tides or when they changed. He drove his car through the railway crossing gates at Kents Bank railway station, continued across the tracks and turned around the back of the station. Pulling off the road by the sea, he parked behind it. He looked for a hiding place.

He knew they would come along soon, so he planned to wait for them to pass, then go back for his car, return to the main road then find the M6. If they chased him that far he could go north or south, they would have to choose.

What Karl didn't know was there had been a spate of rain that week and the River Kent had swelled and the excess water had drained into the bay causing a combination of fast tides, quicksand and shifting channels. The wind-chill was down to zero degrees. No one was hiking this week.

He hid behind an old railway carriage on the bay side of the tracks. What the hell is happening to me, he thought. I look a mess, my hair is dishevelled, I'm all over the place. Two car chases in one day. I rushed out so fast I didn't even think to bring my overcoat.

Then a fog came in from the sea.

He watched Decha's men through the carriage window. Driving slowly past the railway station, then he heard them stop at the end of the road before turning around heading back his way.

The road curves to the right by the railway station and Praves drove carefully past, then stopped the car, turned off the engine and listened. The only sound was the lapping of the waves from the bay. "He is here, I can tell," he said, "The road is too silent, no traffic."

"He was going fast. He could have passed here."

"No, I saw his rear lights turn where the road bends. He's stopped and parked. I'm sure."

"Where could he hide around here?"

They got out and pulled up the collars of their thick coats against the wind. "He's either in his car waiting for us," he pointed towards the coast, "or he's out there hiding."

"He's not dressed for this; he'll freeze if we don't find him soon."

The fog became thicker. They went to the railway station but found it locked for the night.

"Look around the back Atid. I will try that building next door."

Atid walked to the corner of the railway building where the rail crossing gates were up, no more trains tonight. He went through and saw a signpost with a sign for Far Arnside across the bay, and a warning of flood tides and shifting sands. He peered through the fog and saw a car parked a short distance away to the left. At first thought, it probably belonged to the station master. He went closer and looked at the front then saw it was the Monza. He went back and found Praves.

"Prav, you were right he must be hiding here somewhere. I found the car."

"Well done. Any sign of him?"

"No, but he can't be far away."

"Show me the car."

Atid let the way back to Karl's car. The fog was a hindrance, and they had to be careful where they trod. The back of the railway station led straight to the shore and the recent rain had made it soft and spongy. Praves noticed the derelict railway carriage and beckoned Atid towards it.

Karl had managed to squirm down under the carriage by the wheels. There was hardly any light left, and he felt safe there, out of the wind. The sound of the waves lapping against the shore was soothing in a way. Then he heard their footsteps coming, so he made himself as small as possible.

The fog was damp, and it soaked him, the cold was becoming unbearable, the wind chill must be near to zero. He was holding on tightly but his fingers were beginning to numb. The men walked past his hiding place and he thought he could make it back to his car. He slid down and rolled out on the station side of the carriage.

Praves heard a crunching sound as Karl rolled out onto the gravel. He shouted to Atid to get around the other side while he tried to get across underneath. Atid ran around the front of the carriage and saw Karl through the fog, running to his car. He called out to him. "Karit stop, don't run. Wait, we will not hurt you, we only have to take you back."

Karl heard the call and looked back through the gloom. Panicking, he changed his mind, then he changed direction and began running towards the shore. The incoming tide lapped the saltmarsh and the sea suddenly closed in on him from the bay.

The tide rushed into the bay faster than any man can run. The seawater surged up gullies and between sand ridges cutting him off. Waters that came in both in front of and behind trapped him. Then he became disorientated as the fog thickened. He didn't know which way to run, or if he could run, in the water.

Praves and Atid stood at the edge of the marsh calling Karl. They heard Karl calling out for help but the fog hid him from them. They didn't know where he was only that the fog and the sea had taken him.

Seventeen

Al had twisted his knee during the fall and was in a lot of pain. So Toby suggested they go home and rest up for a day or two. They could always get Ashley to find Karl for them, it wasn't over yet. He'd been here nearly a week and he'd promised Jo to be home by now. So after dropping off their hire car at the Hertz office in Chester, they caught a fast train to London's Euston station, stopping at Crewe and Milton Keynes.

Al had slept for most of the journey but Toby had a lot going through his head. It had been a weird week, so much going on. They had almost caught Karl on a few occasions but he'd always managed to get away from them.

He'd looked at his brother affectionately, as he slept on the train and could not for the life of him work out why he had put himself through all the trouble for Tess. He should have told her after Golden Square that they couldn't help her anymore. All that way up to the Lake district then onto wales for what he wasn't sure. He'd let Al sleep in and would confront him in the morning.

Toby couldn't shake the feeling he was missing something. We chased Karl all that way, and Al knew people there. Something was nagging at the back of his head. He hadn't slept well; it confused him and made him angry. He had wanted to say something yesterday, but he'd waited until he had slept on it. This morning he wanted answers. When Al came into the kitchen, he got straight to the point.

"You knew."

"Good morning to you too. Knew what? What do you mean?"

"Come on Al. All the way, every step we took, you knew where he would go. It's as if you planned it all."

"Are you serious we've had a torrid time following him? How could I have planned all that?"

"Maybe not the fights. You couldn't have known there would be any or how they would turn out, but the journey, you pushed him right where you wanted him to go."

"Pushed him. How could I push him? Ashley was telling us where he was. We followed him we didn't push him anywhere."

They were brothers. They had known each other all their lives. Al could never lie to him. So when he blushed then looked him in the eye and smiled. Toby knew he had guessed right.

"Okay let's have it. I know you, Alain, you can't keep a secret for long. It's written all over your face. Tell me I'm wrong if you can. You can't can you?"

"All right, okay, I owe you an explanation."

"Damn right you do. I came to help you in good faith but I got worried about you. You should be in the hospital." He was furious. "I can't believe it, you had it planned all along."

"I'm sorry Toby. You're almost right."

"What do you mean, almost, which part did I miss out?"

"I had no idea he would go to the Lake District."

"Why didn't you tell me?"

"I needed to keep everyone in the dark until I knew we had him."

"Had him, we never had him, did we? We still don't have him. That's not good enough Al I'm your brother you should have trusted me."

"I couldn't trust anybody. The point is nobody knew."

"What about Ashley, is he in on it too?"

"No, only me." Al smiled again. "And Tes."

"Tes! I thought she was the innocent party in all of this. Jesus god almighty Al, I can't believe you didn't trust me."

"Look, will you let me explain?"

"Explain, that's a novel idea. This had better be good. I need a bloody strong drink after this revelation." He marched over to the drinks cabinet and got two glasses and a bottle.

"Put the drink back. I think strong coffee will do."

"I felt something was up, but I couldn't put my finger on it, it's been nagging me for days. No wonder you waited for Sonia to go away."

"Come and sit in the lounge and I'll explain. What time is your flight?"

"Six o'clock tonight. When is Sonia due?"

"Half-past six, it's convenient if you drive me there, I'll wait for her and she can drive us home."

They settled down with a black coffee each, and Al told Toby how it all began.

****

There was a week to go until Christmas. Sonia and I were having breakfast and discussing our trip to Scotland. You know we were going for a short break over the festive period. She is a well-organised person and had sorted out most of the things we needed to pack. The hotel had arranged a black-tie dinner for Christmas day. Boxing Day would be a walk in the Highlands. So, some smart evening wear and some functional winter gear. One big suitcase or our two small carry-ons' plus a suit carrier, we couldn't decide. The house phone stopped us and I went through to the lounge to answer the call.

When I returned I told Sonia who had called.

"That was Tesanee."

"What did she want?"

"To see me."

"When now? why? how long since you spoke?"

"Yes now, not sure, two years."

"Are you going over?"

"I said yes to this afternoon if that's alright, we're not doing anything are we?"

"No, that's fine, wait until after lunch though."

"It won't be much, she didn't sound upset, I reckon she wants to talk about Ashley."

"He's finished college, hasn't he?"

"Ages ago, he's been working a good few years now."

"Time flies and they grow up fast nowadays."

"It does, they do and what's for lunch?"

Tesanee lives in a detached, four-bedroom house on a tree-lined street opposite a village green. The village is in a conservation area of outstanding beauty in the heart of Surrey. According to many estate agents, it is sought after if you could afford it.

I arrived at half-past one, and she answered the doorbell on the first ring.

"Hello, Alain thanks for coming, how's Sonia?"

"She's fine Tes, she sends her love." I gave her a hug. "Merry Christmas, how are things?"

"I'm fine, looking forward to the holidays."

She ushered me into a beautifully decorated lounge. There was a big Christmas tree in the corner by the front window with a couple of presents under it.

"Do you get time off? I thought you were cooking at the Grapes."

"I was, then I helped Romaine for a while, I don't need to work anymore but I can't stay still for a minute, so I help at the community centre."

"That's great Tes at least you are doing something with your life, how's Ashley?"

"Not bad, he's working at a bank now. Can I get you a drink? hot or cold?"

I caught the aroma from the kitchen. "Something smells good; I'll just have water thanks, good for him, he did well at college didn't he."

She left me while she went to fetch the drinks. I had a look round. When she returned, I was admiring a picture of my old mate Alex and their son Ashley when he was younger.

"That's one of the last pictures of them together."

"How long has it been?"

"He's been gone nine years now."

"Such a shame he died so young."

She carried a tray with English scones, jam, cream, a jug of cold water, a glass and a cup of tea for herself. She laid it all on a coffee table.

"Have a drink help yourself to a scone. I know it's Christmas and you usually have mince pies, but I love scones."

"Did you make these?"

"Yes. My first holiday with Alex he took me for afternoon tea at Raffles restaurant in Singapore. I'd never been before it was too posh for my family to afford. That was my first taste of English scones. I've loved them ever since. That was thirty years ago."

"Well, you certainly know how to cook them. Alex told me when he returned to work that year. He was so different then. He'd just met an angel he said. I could see what he meant by the photos."

"You are too kind Alain. I fell for him as well that trip."

"What did you want to talk about?"

"It's sensitive so I hope you don't mind listening."

"Sounds serious. What is it?"

She looked so sad. She reached over and touched my hand. It looked like she wanted to cry.

"I've made a fool of myself."

"I don't think so. You're no fool, Tess."

"I have a personal problem with my partner. He's become a bully and is abusive too. He gets fits of anger and I get scared sometimes."

"He's not hitting you, is he? I'd stop seeing him if I was you, Tes."

"It's not that easy. we've been living together for around eight years now."

"Oh, that is difficult."

"Even though we're not married, we argue about marital

things, the usual, money, sex, just being with him is getting harder. He goes out a lot and when he comes in he's morose. I know something worries him, but he won't tell me."

"It's not financial problems, after the company sale."

"I don't think about that anymore Alain, there's always money when I need it. It's nice not having to worry when I shop now, like when Alex and Ashley were here."

"That's great not to have that weight on your mind."

"Anyway, what I want to ask is if you can help me sort this out."

"The thing is, what's best for you? Do you want him gone or just a quiet word? There are different ways to approach the situation."

"He's also been stealing money from my bank account."

"Oh, my god now that's serious."

"He's been taking a bit each month for around six years."

I was absolutely astounded to be hearing this so it took a moment to register. I sat back in the chair and then asked. "Right, so he's a thief, and you didn't know until now?"

"Yes, I've checked the bank, I searched back through the statements. You can go back seven years you know. It's been disappearing a bit at a time. I know it's him and I want him gone but not until I get it back."

"So how much has he taken?"

"Close to three-quarters of a million."

"What! I had no idea you were that wealthy Tes."

"I did all right from Alex's life insurance but most of it's from the company sale."

"All right, that's an understatement."

"I suppose It is. Yes, I did better than that. The thing is, he's taken a lot of it and I don't know what I can do about it."

"Has he taken it all? And have you been to the police?"

"I'm still a wealthy woman Alain and yes I've told the police, but there's nothing they can do because we have a joint account."

"But that's around ten grand a month. I can't believe it. Oh, Tes how could you let him near Alex's money?"

"It's my money Alain, I had so much I didn't notice it, six years is a long time. Anyway, I loved him at first, still do I suppose."

I took a moment to think. Then I asked her, "Who else knows Tes?"

"Decha knows. I called him and told him about it a while ago."

"Decha, what Alex's mate? That's a name from the past.

"He was my boyfriend before Alex. I introduced them, and they became friends."

"Really, I didn't know that. Were they good friends?"

"Yes, Decha and I were over a long time before I met Alex."

"Has he offered to help?"

"No, he's like the police. He thinks it's a domestic problem. Karl is only spending money from the joint account. All the men from my country think like that. Any money belongs to them."

"Tell me about him, your partner."

She told me about Karl. She met him while she was working at the Grapes. He used to come in a few nights a week and sit at the bar. He liked Asian food and always ordered a meal. She served him, and he flattered her. He asked her out, she said no a few times then she agreed.

No doubt she missed Alex, but she needed some male company and he was obviously, charming. They went to the pictures and different pubs, then sometimes dinner. It took a while because of work commitments. He used to come around, and she'd cook. He didn't know her circumstances and she didn't let on.

"How long after Alex died was this?"

"About a year. It was just me and Ashley until he went to university, I was on my own for a short while."

"Where's Karl from, is he English?"

"We're both from the Philippines, but he's been in England for over twenty years. it's like he is English."

"The Philippines is a big place, Tes. There are thousands of islands. Are his family from Manila?"

"I'm not sure. He talks about his mother a lot, but he never mentions his father."

"I can't believe this, let me think."

"Have a think, and while you're thinking I'll get us some tea."

She left me thinking and went to the kitchen to make the tea. I thought the problem over while I put strawberry jam on my scone, then the cream. She brought back another tray with a teapot, two cups and saucers.

"Ah, is that the Cornish way or the Devon way."

"Excuse me?"

"Jam then cream. I never know which county spreads it that way. Alex told me the two counties think their way is best. Alex liked the cream first then the jam."

"I never thought about it that way before."

"It's nice both ways."

I was sure I already knew the answer to my next question, but I asked her anyway. "Does Ashley know?"

"I don't think so. Sure, he's suspicious of Karl, he always has been but he has had no dealings with my money."

"Have they had any run-ins, arguments?"

"Plenty, Karl thinks Ashely is lazy and Ashley thinks Karl is a show-off, materialistic. Ashley is not a brave person but I don't know what he will do if he finds out."

"Is he, Karl I mean, materialistic?"

"Well, he likes nice things and dresses smartly, drives a nice car."

"What does he do for work? It seems he doesn't need the money though."

"A wealth management company, I don't take much notice. Believe it or not, he's a financial adviser."

"Well, he certainly hasn't advised you, has he. Anyway, what about Ashley, you said he works in a bank now? Doing what?"

"The IT part, I'm not exactly sure what he does but I know when he was at university he wrote a computer program. He's so like his dad, says it got him the job."

Al had finished his drink and wondered if there was anything else he could add.

"May I suggest you don't tell Ashley about this for now? I'm sure he'll find out, but we'll deal with that when we have to. Leave it with me, I'll be back. You must be patient though, play the innocent."

I had an idea what I wanted to do, but I needed to think of a way to include Ashley, so he doesn't get wind of it, no point him going off half-cocked. I stood up to leave. Tes rose to see me out then she leaned forward and gave me a quick kiss on the cheek.

"Thanks, Alain, I appreciate this. You were a great friend to Alex. Give my love to Sonia."

"Thanks, Tes, I'll be in touch."

****

I sat in the car a few moments, my mind whirring. Tesanee's tale had wrenched my gut. The heartbreak of losing Alex and the worry for Ashley being in his most important exam stage.

Another thought had struck me, what if there was no money, he could have spent it all? I drove in a foggy daze most of the way home.

When I arrived, Sonia took one look at my face and asked. "Everything all right? How is she?"

"She looks well."

"But?"

"Oh, you always know something's up."

"Women's intuition."

"She's got a problem with her man. She's asked for my help."

"And?"

"I'm going to help her."

"Alain! it's Christmas and we're going away for a week."

"I know I'm not going to help until after Christmas, maybe when you go to Spain."

It was at the front of my mind now, I had something to do. After three months without a meaningful job, I need this.

****

Toby was engrossed with Al's story so far and hadn't spoken since he'd started. He had finished his coffee though, a while ago, but he didn't want to disturb the flow of the tale. Now he needed a break to digest what he'd heard.

"Hang on a minute while I get a stronger drink. Want one?"

"Yes, go on, same as you. I need to wet my whistle so to speak."

Toby poured them both then went in search of something to nibble on. He found a packet of biscuits and when he returned, he asked.

"So, you were going to help her all along. Did you two have a plan?"

"I'm sorry if this is a long story. It was my plan, but it didn't go well at first."

"You don't say?"

He settled back down to hear the rest.

Eighteen

Al cleared his throat and continued.

I thought and thought and surfed and thought some more over the weekend. Then on Monday I called Tesanee and arranged another meeting. I had seen something on my last visit and I wanted confirmation.

Sonia was on my case straight away. "You said you would not help her until after Christmas."

"I know, but I saw something when I was there and I need to ask her about it."

"You promised."

"I'll only be an hour. I'll be back before lunch."

"You'd better be I have plans for today."

"Don't get me wrong I didn't plan this but I may have to do some things before we go."

"I know you have been bored at home recently, but please don't spend all week on this."

"I'll try to keep it low key."

No chance. This had piqued my interest, and I wanted to get stuck in.

On the way over I had to get my mind straight about a few things. I had plenty of questions to ask her. My main worries were.

We need to get him to pay her back.

The problems are, he's taken a long time to steal it so he could have been spending it during that time.

If he's still got it, he will not want to pay it back easily.
We can't accuse him either, because of the joint account.
I expect she'll want him gone as well.
She said she still loved him though.

When I arrived she was expecting me to tell her how I planned to help. She led me through to the lounge again. I noticed they had added more presents to the pile under the tree. The picture of Alex and Ashley was in the same place. I picked it up to get a closer look. I was looking beyond them though. Someone had taken it in the lounge and on the coffee table behind was a stamp album laying open. Tes went to get drinks.

She came back and reminded me.

"I don't want him hurt I want him to pay back what he's taken and then leave me alone."

I was still trying to zoom my eyesight at the book. Trying to make out the stamps when I answered.

"How long has Ashley been collecting stamps?"

"He doesn't. It was Alex who collected stamps."

"There's a book on the table in the photograph."

"I know. Alex was proud of his collection. He tried to get Ashley interested but you know what children are like they think anything their parents did is boring."

"I didn't know he was a collector."

"He started when he was a boy. His father liked to dabble, many of his were expensive. Alex was old school all his life."

"Have you still got the stamp album?"

"Yes, I kept it up for a few months after Alex went. Nothing valuable you know just lifted from letters Ashley wasn't interested, it's in the attic. We kept a few boxes of Alex's things, just keepsakes. Do you want to see it?"

"Sometimes maybe, not now. I need to ask you something."

"Go ahead what is it."

"You mentioned Alex and Decha were friends, so does Ashley know Decha as well?"

"Of course, they are quite close. Since Alex, he has turned to Decha as a father figure. Karl resents him, but Ashley doesn't like Karl much."

I had an inkling of an idea.

"Right I'm joining the dots. Decha seems to be in the middle here. He knows Ashley and through you, he knows Karl too. Karl and Ashley don't get on. Ashley turns to Decha for support."

"Yes, they all know each other."

"Has Decha visited when Karl was home?"

"No, I won't have Decha in the house. He comes to pick up Ashley and they go out together. Karl is sometimes here. He keeps out of the way though."

My idea just ballooned into something much larger.

"Why is Decha not welcome here, Tes?"

"It's a sad, unhappy love affair so I'll keep it short. He didn't treat me well when we were going out. Decha is a powerful man, and he's always been full of himself, he had worked his way up from a street urchin to be the leader of a local gang and I was supposed to be his 'Beautiful Rose' as he put it.

"The thing is, I wasn't treated like one. Do this do that, run here run there. He wanted to have the biggest gang, so he surrounded himself with young lads who idolised him. Like he was collecting them. I was glad when he dumped me."

"I'm sorry to hear that. So, he was a gang leader. It makes me think he probably still is. Just a thought, you said he collected things does he collect other things as well?"

"Well I suppose so, Alex always showed him his latest stamp. Whenever they were together, he always showed interest."

"Okay, I have an idea, are you sure you don't want to hurt him?"

"Yes, I've already said that is what I want."

"So, we take a softly, softly approach. We don't have to accuse him, maybe we could get him to spend it."

It shocked Tes. "What! I want the money back not for him to spend it. We both lose that way?"

"Not necessarily. If we could tempt him to buy something that's hard for him to resist."

"Like what?" She was far from convinced. "I don't understand that's still spending it."

"On something he knows is worth more than the asking price. We will sell it to him. Through an intermediary."

"You mean trick him into buying something he can sell on for say, twice the money he paid."

"That's the idea yes."

"What have we got that would interest him?"

"We have nothing, yet, we'll make something up, if he's into stealing money, my bet is he'll want property too. It will be too good for him to resist." She looked thoughtful, I could tell she was sceptical.

I needed to know more about Karl. Where did he come from and why here?

"How can I find out more about him Tes?"

"Well, I told you we both come from Singapore didn't I."

"Yes, I know that."

"How about Decha? I might not like him but he's the only person here that I know from home. He knows a lot of the old folk, he might know how to find out more about Karl and he lives in London now."

"I'd like to leave him out for now but it's somewhere to start. Do you still have contact with him?"

"I haven't spoken to him for a few years, but I've kept his phone number."

She left me alone again while she went to get it. I was deep in thought when she returned with a business card.

"Here is the last number I have for him. It's his mobile so I hope he's still using it. There's an address on there."

"Thanks, I'll give him a call later. Anything else to help with Karl?"

"I can't think of anything. You're best asking Ashley about Decha he kept in touch more than me."

"I don't want to involve Ashley either but if he can put me in touch with Decha, I suppose it will be ok."

"He's known him all his life. He was a young child when he

met him but Decha visited here when he came to England and got friendly with Ashley again."

I had stopped listening for a moment. I remembered Decha from twenty years ago and I also remembered he had been in prison. He'd been working as an office cleaner in Singapore when he became involved in a car accident. The police had searched the car and found a stack of money in a pouch, he was in trouble. He couldn't explain it away, and because with his job, he shouldn't be carrying so much money. Gambling is common in that country but still, they confiscated the money and sent him to prison.

I focused again as Tesanee was still talking. "Remember, Ashley had lost his father and Alex and Decha were quite close back in the day. Alex and Decha were the same age, and he was always around our place. He liked Ashley, he used to bring him small gifts back then, Ashley remembered him and respected him."

That made me think. Maybe Ashley could help me get under Karl's skin.

I went home and did some more internet surfing. My Idea was to put something under his nose that he couldn't resist. Decha seemed to be at the heart of this, he kept popping up.

Tesanee would need to bring out all her old acting skills. I knew she was capable of fooling him as she had been in an amateur dramatics group before Alex had met her. She gave it up when they came to England.

****

"Excuse me a minute Toby, I need a break."

Al left the room and Toby wondered if he'd worked out what was coming next. He couldn't believe the story so far. It seemed farfetched, but he wanted to hear the rest now.

Al returned from the toilet and poured them both another drink.

"So you're thinking Decha is at the back of all this, Is that right?"

"Let me tell you the rest, then you can judge for yourself okay."

"I'm all ears." Toby sniggered and was on the edge of his seat.

****

My first call was to an old friend.

"Hi Jeff, how have you been keeping. How's Joyce?"

"Hi Alain, we're doing well thanks, long time no see. How's Sonia?"

"We're okay too, thanks. Sorry to bother you at home."

"No, bother what can I do for you?"

"Does your daughter still work at that bank in Grand Cayman?"

"Yes, why?"

"Can she open accounts?"

"Whoa, I wasn't expecting that, I thought you wanted a holiday or something. I think she can, why, who needs one?"

"I do; can you find out what's required without having to go there?"

"Have you won the lottery or robbed a bank? Don't tell me, I'll ask her this evening its five hours behind us over there."

"Thanks, Jeff, I'm planning a trip up north soon, so I'll try to stop by."

"I hope to see you. When were you thinking of coming?"

"In the new year. Early January, it's bound to be snowing though."

"More than likely, I'll call you back when I know more. Love to Sonia."

My second call to a new friend.

"Hi Fritz, how's Denise?"

The man who answered spoke with a Swiss-German accent "Hello Alain, Wie geht es dir Denise ist gut."

"English Fritz, can you speak English please?"

"Sorry Alain, I forgot you don't speak German. How are you, Denise is good."

"We're both all right thanks. I need a favour, Fritz."

Fritz had been a freight train driver in his younger days but had studied to be an accountant at the Open University. He was so good at it he eventually became the manager of a Swiss bank in Bern.

"What can I do for you, my friend?"

"I would like to open an account at your branch."

"I can do that, but you will need to come here to register your details.

"Oh, come on Fritz can't you open it for me."

"I can create an account online, but it will not become active until I run the usual checks and copy your passport."

"How long do the checks take?"

"Not long we can do it in a day."

"That's good. Create the account please and I'll come over for a day to go through the formalities."

"Fine let me know when you are coming, and I'll arrange dinner with Denise."

"Right I'll get back to you."

****

"You said you were planning a trip up north. Was it for this?" Toby asked.

"No, that was just for conversation. I said I had no idea about the Lake District, then."

"Okay, but you knew about Decha. How did you find out about his vault under Golden Square?"

"That was Fraser."

"*Fraser*, who the hell is Fraser?"

"He's a mate of mine from work."

"I'm losing count of the people who knew about this. Everyone except me."

"That's not true. They only played a small part and they don't know about each other. You'll soon find out."

****

That was my third and last call. He answered at the second ring. "Al, what's up mate?"

"Hi Fraser, are you free this afternoon I have something for you?"

"Not much going on so close to Christmas Al. You know our business."

"Right I'll be at the usual bar around three. See you there."

"No problem."

I was getting somewhere and loving it. Ideas were flooding out of me. Karl Hurnston didn't know what was coming and even if he did, he would not like it.

At three that afternoon, I entered the All-Bar-One in Holborn and saw Fraser propping up the bar with a pint of amber liquid in his hand. He was chatting to a nice-looking woman serving behind the bar.

Fraser had a forgettable face, he was average in clothes size. He had fair hair, cut short, and a clipped moustache. He had no distinguishable marks and everyone forgot him the moment he left them. He suited my purposes perfectly.

I patted him on the shoulder "Watcha."

He turned my way then said to his new friend.

"Please, will you excuse me my friend is here to drag me away?"

"Nice talking to you." Then she turned to me. "What can I get you, sir?"

"A pint of lager please." She went off to pour it.

Fraser shook my hand. "Hi Al, what's up this is short notice isn't it."

The barmaid came back with my drink and I paid for them.

I took him by the arm. "Let's find a table away from the bar, shall we." We chose one at the back near the wall. "You're not busy, are you?"

"As I said, not much location work required around Christmas so I'm enjoying a well-earned rest."

"Perfect. I'm researching someone and I need a background check." I gave him a printed copy of the business card that Tesanee had given me. "The guy has an office in Soho. The postcode looks like it's near Golden Square, could be on it."

"Okay, what kind of background check?"

"Anything you can find would help. What business is he involved in? Is it legit, is he married, children, home address? The lot."

"Not too difficult nowadays. Have you tried the internet?"

"I'm kind of busy and in a hurry too."

"So immediate start then?"

"Yes please."

"Does it pay?"

"Of course, the usual hourly rate."

"I'm all yours I'll keep you informed as usual."

"Good. Anyway, how's life? How's Margaret?"

"She's okay, always busy. You know what it's like. Our job takes me away a lot, and she's been patient with me. She's a great housekeeper too. Looks after the place as I'm away so much."

"Yes, I know. We are going to Scotland for Christmas so anything you can come up with this week will be great."

"Nice idea. Scotland I mean, we thought about doing that once but we never got around to organising it. Then before you know it it's too late."

"Okay well, I can't stay so keep in touch and have a great Christmas. I'll talk to you later."

We finished our drinks, and I left him to contemplate where to start.

****

I arrived home and went straight to my laptop to go through my ideas again, just to be clear. I booked a seat on the mid-morning Swissair flight from Heathrow to Bern. Then I emailed Fritz to say I would arrive tomorrow lunchtime, but it would be a flying visit and I couldn't stay for dinner.

I contemplated my next move. The internet is a great thing, and I soon found what I wanted and set about creating a false trail for Karl to latch onto. I made copies of pictures, printed brochures and leaflets. I created a dummy website filled it with worthless information and published it. It all sounded legitimate and looked authentic. I was convinced I created the perfect scenario. Now I had to plant it under his nose.

I called in a favour from one of my oldest friends. I asked when he was working his favourite hobby again. He said in the middle of January. I asked him to text me the date.

Time to call Tesanee again.

"Hi Tes, I'm ready, is it all right to come over and kick this off?"

"I can't believe your timing. Karl is staying in London for a few days. He's got a big deal going down and needs to work all hours completing it before Christmas."

"Right, I'll be over first thing. I've got a lot of explaining to do. See you tomorrow."

Nineteen

Next day I arrived early armed with a folder full of papers and my laptop. Tes let me in and we set up in her dining room.

"We will have to keep this short I have a plane to catch at Heathrow this morning. I'm going straight from here."

"No problem, what have you got?"

I showed her the leaflets and explained the ideas. She knew straight away what she had to do. I took her through the web pages of the dummy site until she knew it by heart. She would have to sell the idea to Karl in such a way as he thought it was something she really wanted and was going to buy.

We hoped he would panic when he realised she didn't have the funds, but she thought she did. He would either put it back or offer to help her purchase it.

Tes left the brochures, and a few leaflets around the house, on the coffee table, in the kitchen. If he mentioned anything about them, she would show enthusiasm and say she was extremely interested in purchasing. If not, she would show him and ask for his advice. My guess was he wouldn't want to give any money back.

There was no point hiding them from Ashley and it would add to the drama if he became interested too. Would he tell his 'Uncle' Decha though?

I was most insistent. "It's important to point out it's the one called 'The Whole Country is Red'."

"I understand."

"Sonia and I are going to Scotland for Christmas, so I won't

163

be contactable. Have a great Christmas with Ashley give him my regards and I'll see you in the new year."

"You too, love to Sonia."

I drove straight to Heathrow, parked in the short-stay car park and caught my Swissair flight to Bern. I took a taxi from the airport straight to Fritz's office. Thankfully, they accepted euros as I hadn't had time to get any Swiss francs. I always had euros as my job took me to Europe most of the time.

It was only the second time I had set foot in Switzerland though. It had been snowing, and that day was cold. The wind was going right through me. Still, the seasonal decorations around the streets looked magical. They had switched the Christmas lights on and lit up the main street. Shame I didn't have time to get a good look round.

He welcomed me like a long-lost friend with a bear hug. Then he drove us to a traditional Swiss restaurant called Da Edelweiss for lunch. The menu was in German so I let Fritz order. He chose open sandwiches with everything I could think of on them. Whilst eating he explained what the bank needed. It wouldn't be a problem as I had my passport, driving license and a utility bill.

After lunch, he took me to the bank, and I signed the forms for my new Swiss bank account and paid in a couple of thousand euros. It was a flying visit, so he was kind enough to drop me straight back to the airport. I thanked him, sent my regards to his wife Denise then flew home for dinner.

The day so far had been hectic, but it wasn't over yet. That evening Jeff called me. "Hi, Alain how was your day?"

"Hello, Jeff. It's been busy; I've been to Bern. Not been home long. Did you speak to your daughter?"

"You get around. But yes, I did, and she's willing to open the account if you sent all your documents via a secure link. She will email you with the website she uses and a password for protection."

"That's great Jeff. I can't thank you enough. This is going to help no end."

"Right, well you should get the email soon. If you haven't received it by now. Check your spam box."

"I haven't checked for a while. I usually get a message on my phone but thanks, anyway."

"I hope you can stop and see us on your way to the Lakes next month."

"I'll try. You know how it is I've got a hectic lifestyle."

"Have a great Christmas and love to Sonia. See you soon."

I hoped all this effort was worth it, but I was ready for a good night's sleep.

The next morning, I checked my emails and found the one from Jeff's daughter. All she needed was the same details I'd given Fritz. Thankfully he'd suggested I get more copies. So he'd obliged, and I had a set ready made for her. There was a link to a secure website, so I could upload the documents straight away. I asked her to link the new account to the one I'd opened yesterday in Bern.

Then Sonia and I went to Scotland and had a great short break. In fact, it was one of the best Christmas's I could remember.

Ashley came to visit Tesanee a few days later and saw the article on the kitchen worktop. He asked her about it and she told him it was something to remind her of his dad. He thought she was wasting her money and advised her not to buy it, and asked his mum if it involved Karl. She told him he didn't know about it yet. The question was would he tell Decha. I'd gambled that he wouldn't think to involve him. I hoped not at least.

Karl came home with Christmas presents. He went in the lounge, put them under the tree, sat down and his eyes landed on the pamphlet on the coffee table. He flicked through the pages, then took it into the kitchen to ask Tesanee about it. She showed him the website with more details. When she told him what she was going to buy, he knew he was in trouble. She couldn't afford it, but she didn't know. With the money he'd taken she could. How was he going to change her mind?

Tesanee had known Karl long enough to see the change in him. She knew his mind was whirring, trying to make sense out of it. She started to believe the plan would work. She made light of it saying she was waiting until next year because she wanted to enjoy Christmas together. Ashely was coming over Christmas day.

They didn't talk about it anymore until after the festive period when she brought up the subject again. She was going to buy it as a new year present for herself. She considered it a wise investment.

****

I came home after Christmas and left Tesanee to it. I waited for her to contact me with any problems or if Karl had taken the bait. On the second of January Karl left for work and never returned.

In the meantime, I had a few dozen emails to get through. Mostly junk, but one was from Fraser. He wanted to meet to discuss his progress and also give me an invoice.

I called him and arranged to meet him the next day. We met in the same bar and he had a ton of information for me.

"Watcha, this is just a first report. Tell me if you want me to keep at it after I've told you what I know."

"Cheers for this." We clinked glasses. "Go ahead."

"To start with his place is not on Golden Square. It's under Golden Square. He's running a gentlemen's club. There is an office, but it's not used much he keeps his private things there."

"Under the Square. Really? Who would guess there is a room under the Square? How did you find out?"

"Looked it up online, it was an old air raid shelter, they used it until 1945 then closed it up. He reopened it and turned it into a trendy place with guys and exotic dancers. He rents it off the Westminster Council."

"Well done. Any more interesting little gems?"

"He has an air-conditioned vault down there too."

"You have been busy. How do you do it?"

"I went there and watched from a café across the square for a couple of hours, saw a few people coming and going and noted them down. I went back the next day and this Asian-looking couple came into the café. They bought green tea each and talked for a short while. I watched and waited then got lucky. The guy left on his own, so I followed him.

"He didn't go far, just to the nearest pub, where he sat at the bar and ordered a bottle of Japanese beer. I sat close to him, ordered the same beer, then started chatting. As you do. I started complaining about my work and asked him if he was happy at his job. He said he wasn't happy at first then he shut up and turned away. I didn't give up and tried to get him to say why."

"Amazing! You have the knack of befriending people that I couldn't learn."

"He wasn't happy that I wanted information about his boss, but he smiled at my offer of another beer. Turns out he works in the club and had the afternoon off. So, after a few more drinks he started to tell all."

"Alcohol usually works."

"I played the lonely soul. Anyway, totally disillusioned, he works for a bully, wants to leave but thinks he'll be punished if he does. He told me a few personal things about his boss. He knew he shouldn't but he couldn't shut up once he'd had a few and got started. He went on to tell me."

"Go on."

"He lords over everyone who works for him. Constantly telling them to work harder. They all work long hours, but he doesn't care. Most of them are illegally here so they can't do anything about it. It's like he's the leader of a very posh gang. Also, there's a rumour he's been to prison for money laundering. Not here but wherever he comes from. Which I think is the Far East. He's pretty smart with his money and only buys things as an investment, always wants more, you know, never has enough."

"Okay thanks, this is all helpful, anything else?"

"The vault is full of precious antiques. Not big stuff, Old jewellery, watches, cut glass. Stuff like that, he's got loads of rare stamps in glass boxes. A few of them worth a small fortune, this guy reckons. He boasts about them all the time and shows them off to his clients. I've written all this down and I'll email it to you later. Have you spoken to Morgan?"

"Yes, I called him. Thanks Fraser, you've done a great job. Add your invoice to the email."

****

Toby had sat patiently listening to Al's story.

"The following week Ashley came into the café. That's when I called you. Come on I'm famished let's have lunch."

They carried on talking while preparing lunch.

"That is an unbelievable story. So, you knew Decha's surname even though you told him you didn't."

"I didn't want him to think I'd worked him out. That I knew what he was doing with Tes."

"And you knew he was a nasty piece of work. What did you think he was doing with Tes?"

"He loved her and always has. Well, maybe not loved so much, more of an obsession. It was only my assumption at first but the more I talked with her and Ashley I knew he would never let her go.

He's a collector, and he didn't want to lose his 'Beautiful Rose' as he called her. I bet he hated it when she finished with him. Even more when she met Alex, a rich Englishman who would take her away to another country. So, he made friends with Alex then visited them a lot. He was always at their house when I was there. Now he could keep her close even though she was married to Alex he was always there."

"So, all this chasing Karl was to get at Decha. Was it?"

"When Ashley asked me to help out it completely threw me. I had to help him or he would have got someone else."

168

"True, he was determined to get his mum's money back."

"I didn't expect Karl to be so angry and spiteful though."

"Good job you called me."

"Yes, great idea. I'd worked out Karl was related to Decha and I think he sent him here to be his eyes on the ground if you like until he could come himself. Karl courted Tes and eventually moved in with her. My guess was he reported back to his uncle about everything she was doing on a regular basis."

"That's all conjecture on your part."

"It was at first but when I found out he collected things it made me think why not people. He used Ashley as an excuse to keep in touch. When he came to England, he tried to visit her, but she wouldn't see him. So, he got close to Ashely again and effectively took over from Alex."

"Did you know Karl was going to buy that stamp?"

"Of course I did, It was my idea. The whole auction thing was my idea."

"You're a crafty bastard. I was right, you made sure he would go to that auction. You planned the whole trip. How did you know he would go for it though?"

"It was a gamble, but Tes told me he had taken one of my pamphlets. So, I was pretty sure he had thought he could get it before her. I knew she wasn't going, so I made sure if he showed an interest, I would be the first to know. One of the rules of an auction is that you must register your bank details before you can bid. I had the registrar text me the moment Karl's details arrived."

"You have got to be joking. How do you know the registrar?"

"Remember that call I made to one of my oldest friends. That was the registrar, a guy called Morgan Hill."

"So, Fraser knows Morgan as well. I can't believe this. Did you meet him on location somewhere?"

"Yes, I've known him for about thirty years. He works for the same company as me. He does it part-time, as a hobby. I went to his stag do, up in Barrow. That's where I met Sonia."

"Sonia was there?"

"Yes, I told you, she comes from there. I went up with a few of Morgan's mates. There were six of us going to the wedding. We went to Sidings disco the night before. Morgan was marrying Della, who knew Hannah, and that's where we met Sonia and Eleanor and their mates."

"So, Sonia knows Hannah and Eleanor."

"Yes, they were mates back then."

"I thought you and Hannah looked too close. Sorry, I'm just trying to take all this in. I forgot Sonia comes from there, I should have remembered that. I often wondered where you two met though, but I wouldn't have guessed that part of the country. I thought you met down here. She's lost most of her northern accent. Did you know everyone at the auction?"

"No, not everyone just the bidders for Lot 117, and Morgan. They were part of the scam."

"Amazing! All that set-up and it was a gamble he would go for it. What about any other bidders? You didn't know if someone else wanted it."

"The main brochures didn't have the stamp in it. Just the few I had printed, and we added the lot on the day, so all other bidders didn't know about it."

"You seemed to have thought of everything but what about Ashley?"

"When he asked me to help, I had to improvise."

"So, you agreed and called me. Still, you hoped he would end up at the auction."

"That was the plan but when he went up north, I thought he had other ideas."

"So, a roundabout route."

"Greed takes over Toby. Karl saw an opportunity to make more money off the back of it and he took it. What made you suspect anything was up?"

"It began at the auction. I wondered why he had gone there. It seemed odd, out of the way. I didn't know about the auction of course until we arrived. Then I thought we had finally caught up with him and had him cornered. We would stop him on his way out. I thought that was our job done. I wanted to shake it out of him.

"Then when he started bidding, and it kept going up, I got confused. You let him carry on. It was going to cost him a fortune and you let him carry on raising the bid."

Al smiled again. "Well, I wanted it to go as high as possible. Fraser was one of the other bidders. He sat two rows in front of Karl and the lady on the phone was a friend of Hannah. I wanted him to spend it all."

"Why? We are supposed to get Tes her money back not for him to spend it on a stupid stamp."

"It's not a stupid stamp it is actually worth what he paid for it. It's extremely rare. There are only a few left in the world."

"Really, I wouldn't have guessed. Did Ashley know about the auction?"

"Tes said he saw the magazine but I'm not sure if he knew Karl would go. Maybe when he found out Karl was in Wales, he put two and two together."

"But how did you know he would buy that stamp?"

"We planted it in his head."

A light came on inside Toby's head. "Hold on do you mean he bought it from you?"

"Exactly. Now you're getting it."

"What about the stamp was it real?"

"No."

"Hold on, where's the money, Al?"

"Look, Ashley asked me to help, and he got what he wanted, so did Tes. We got her money back, and that's what they both wanted."

"That's not what I asked. She gets hers but that's not all of it though is it?"

"After expenses for the team, the rest is split. Half is yours. You've earnt it."

"I can't believe it. This has never happened in my life before." He checked his watch and realised he still had Al's fancy video watch.

He took it off and replaced it with his own. "Here you had better have this back, come on I've got to get to the airport."

Toby forced himself into the car again and drove them to Gatwick. He parked in the car park this time. In the departure hall Al cringed as he hugged him, then shook his hand and said he would call him when he arrived home. As he walked away, he wondered if it had all been worth the trip, according to Al it had. It certainly hadn't been a holiday.

Al went through to the arrivals lounge and found a café. He ordered coffee and sat pondering over the last week while he waited for Sonia and Jess to arrive. He was waiting by the arrival doors as they walked through.

"Oh my god, what has happened to you."

"Hi, Sonia, hi Jess, could you drive us back please darling? I haven't managed to do much work on your list."

Twenty

The Whole Country is Red

The Whole Country is Red is a valuable Chinese stamp issued in 1968.

It is a modern stamp commissioned by Chairman Mao to represent communism over the whole of China. But by a complete error, the designer left Taiwan in white. This was massively controversial – he thought he would be going to prison for treason. The stamp was hurriedly recalled

The stamp has such a name due to a slogan that it contains. The item represents Mao's enormous political revolution that imposed China's commitment to Communism. The stamp strengthened that notion by declaring the phrase: 'The whole country is red'. It featured an army of smiling Chinese citizens holding Mao's Little Red Book, *a symbol of communism. Although the overall design of this philatelic item was made in red colour, the small island of Taiwan, to the right, was left in white. That is why this stamp is so valuable, as it contains a design mistake! Once the mistake was detected, the stamp was quickly withdrawn from the market. It is not known how many error stamps are left, but they are definitely extremely rare.*

Sothebys is a guesthouse in Wales and is not connected in any way to Sotheby's Auction House.

Acknowledgements

I would like to thank everyone who read the manuscript and offered suggestions for improvements. A massive thank you to my wife Sharon and all five of our children who have put up with me spending every spare moment talking about and writing it. There are also many others to thank for their support.

A big thank you to everyone at Authoright for editing, typesetting, cover design and publishing the manuscript.

Any mistakes, it goes without saying, are entirely my own.

About the Author

Dennis was born and raised in South London, UK, where his parents, both avid readers, made a habit of bringing home crime, thriller and suspense novels, instilling in Dennis a love of reading from a very early age. He and his father used to pass any book they read onto each other.

Dennis spent many years as an engineering designer particularly the oil and gas industry, hence the few years in the oil rich Arabian gulf where his first story is set, before deciding what he really wanted to do was write.

He realised the most satisfying way to achieve this would be by starting with his own story. So for the next eighteen months Dennis spent his days working at his regular job and his lunchtimes, evenings and weekends writing his first book.

Prisoner in Al-Khobar was the result.

Dennis lives in Surrey with his wife. He is currently hard at work on his third book, another novel this time.

9 781913 136154